SPEAK
— *to the* —
STORMS

A NOVEL

Ben Williams

"Blessed are the peacemakers,
for they shall be called sons of God."

Matthew 5:9

Ben Williams

brotherbenwilliams@gmail.com.

Cover design by Fallon Bradford.
Author photo by Ed Bolt.

One

Marcus Paver grew up in a stormy world. His country was edging toward civil war. He didn't want to get caught in the crossfire, and he didn't want that for his family or friends either.

In fourth grade Marcus and his best friend rushed out the door of their Folsom, California school for recess. Marcus nudged Hunter. "Let's do the crossbars."

Hunter answered, "Yeah, we'll show these kids who's got the muscles."

They took their place at the back of the line. A younger girl missed a bar halfway across and dropped to the artificial turf. The two boys gave each other a knowing look. That afternoon Marcus felt as secure as a caterpillar in a cocoon. He and Hunter and a hundred other kids scampered around their peaceful playground. The chatter and laughter and occasional shouts of their classmates bounced off the walls that surrounded them on three sides.

Then suddenly a bizarre, foreign noise pierced the cocoon from the side that was open to the street. Marcus caught on first and reacted by primal instinct. In a nosedive toward the turf, he screamed, "Get down!"

Hunter followed like the next domino in line.

Gunfire erupted on the street where two local would-be world-changers found each other and aimed to make their voices heard at the end of their pistols. The sound of squealing tires followed three loud blasts.

Marcus and Hunter, the students and teachers all lay flat and frightened as two vehicles dashed their radicalized drivers away. The amateur shooters were lousy shots. They left no blood out on the street. Nor did any of their flying lead accidently hit any of the children. Still, every kid, every parent, everyone involved experienced some degree of inner trauma, including Marcus Paver.

That night, in the security of their home, his mother comforted him as best she could. Bedtime came. Feeling more vulnerable than secure, the nine-year-old lay awake, worrying. He eventually drifted off to sleep and dreamed he was at the lake at the edge of town. He smiled in his sleep as he watched the peaceful reflection of the afternoon sky on that smooth natural mirror.

Then suddenly a tornado-like whirlwind thrashed up the surface of the water and turned the appealing scene into a nightmare. Marcus saw his friend in a puny boat with dark waves crashing over its sides. "Hunter, I'm coming," he yelled, but he couldn't break himself free from invisible cords that seemed to hold him back.

Yet sometimes in dreams the unexpected, inexplicable happens, as it also does in life. Young Marcus broke loose and rose with courage and faith. With a voice of authority not often heard from a nine-year-old, he commanded the wind.

"Stop!"

And it did.

The water returned to glass. Hunter paddled safely to shore. Marcus stood there thinking, "I did it. I'm just a kid, but I told the storm to stop, and it did."

He woke up, and the frustrating parts of his dream naturally blended with the playground shock he witnessed the day before. He thought, Someday I'll be tall and strong, and I'll command the shooters to stop shooting. As he grew up, the desire to speak to storms grew within him.

Two

Seven years later Marcus inwardly cheered when the bell signaled the end of his sociology class at Folsom High and the end of the school day. Now a junior, Marcus hummed a happy tune as he walked down the hall and stepped through the glass doors, joining the crush of students spilling onto the sidewalk. A mild rumble of thunder sounded in the distance, and the sweet aroma of a possible afternoon rain shower filled the air.

A kid he knew stepped up beside him and asked, "How's your Indie folk band doing? I've heard good things."

Marcus answered, "We're doing great, playing a lot, writing some tunes. Yeah!"

"I heard you write most of the songs. Very creative!"

Marcus responded sincerely, "Thanks! You headed this way?"

"Yeah."

The two started down the sidewalk away from school. They walked a block, turned a corner and found themselves on the edge of a dozen students encircled around a fist fight. They stopped. With a perplexed look on his face, Marcus turned toward his friend and questioned in a quiet voice, "Why are these people so quick to pick fights?"

Then, smash! Another punch landed on the smooth young skin of the smaller guy's jaw. Marcus cringed but camouflaged his sympathy, thinking, *I don't want this bunch to think I'm soft.* Another fist hammered into the weakened opponent's bludgeoned face and more blood and other fluids oozed out. Marcus decided he'd had enough.

Before leaving, he leaned over to his partner and offered a theory. "Maybe he wants to toughen up and become a revolutionary. He thinks one of these heroically insane causes these days needs his help." His friend shrugged his shoulders. As Marcus trudged down the street, the echoes of classmates alternately whimpering and then cheering for the combatants faded away.

The light rain arrived, and another classmate eased by in his aging Chevy pickup. He cracked open his passenger side window. "Wanna get out of this rain?" Marcus lifted himself out of his reflective mood enough to reply, "Oh, hey, man. Thanks, but no. I can walk."

With a concerned look, the young driver asked, "You OK?"

"Yeah, sure," Marcus replied in a fake self-confident voice.

The guy asked, "Is the band playing somewhere tonight?"

With real confidence Marcus affirmed, "We are!"

"Where?"

"The hotel."

"Knock 'em dead!"

"Thanks."

He began the two-mile trek home and thought, *Great. "Knock 'em dead!"*

Two blocks later he remembered a word of advice from his uncle. "A long walk is a good opportunity to turn things over in your head." Marcus thought, *I wonder why there's so much fighting at school and everywhere else.*

He angled out past Willow Hill Reservoir. The rain and wind were already subsiding, and the small lake mirrored the artwork of the sun as it peeked through the parting clouds. He thought, *I heard a story about a storm that stopped unexpectedly. It was at Vacation Bible School when Mom dropped me off. Seems like Jesus told a violent wind to settle down, and it did.*

As he walked away from the lake, he remembered an old movie he watched with his mom. *It was that one about the beauty queen pageant. The host asked that silly character what she would do for humanity. She was going to help bring about world peace. Yeah, right. World peace. Fictional fantasy! Why even bother to think about it?*

He plodded on and battled the video images in his mind of a country edging into civil war. He told himself, *I wish someone could turn this country in a better direction.*

Three

Marcus carried his mixed bag of thoughts and feelings the rest of the way home. He shuffled through the front door into the living room of the family's modest suburban house. Ark, the family Beagle-mix met him with a slobbery lick on his hand.

Mom called from the kitchen. "Is that you, Markie?"

"It's Marcus," he replied with his customary hint of irritation.

"Okay, Bubba."

"Mom!"

"Are you going to come in here and help me put these groceries away?"

Her boy walked through the kitchen door, not really a boy anymore. Though fairly reserved, a noticeable presence had developed about him. He was slender, but by no means weak. He kept his medium length hair in style but on the shaggy side. He was good-looking with an intelligent, compassionate face that had recently started to need a regular shave.

His mom, Gloria Paver had just breezed in from work and appeared windblown. She said, "I'm yearning to know if The Yearning is playing somewhere tonight. And why are you all wet?"

The Yearning's guitarist and main songwriter responded, "It was sprinkling, and I walked home. We'll be at the hotel."

Gloria said, "It's exciting that you guys get to play there so often! My friend at work said our historic hotel has become the trendiest showcase for local bands. So, you know I'm proud of you, Son, but even Indie folk stars need to get their homework done. Do it, and then go knock their musical socks off." Marcus nodded and descended the stairs to the family room. He navigated around the pool table, turned on the lamp next to the old, brown, worn-out, easy chair and settled in.

The assigned chapter in his sociology book dealt with social ills that never seem to go away. It fit his recent mindset. Marcus, along with all sixteen-year-old Americans, could not ignore the trouble brewing around the country. Earlier in the day a classmate said a military draft might start up. He heard it would reach down to eighteen-year-old boys and twenty-year-old girls. Deferments would be slightly more lenient for girls.

The section in his book was titled, "Man's Inhumanity to Man." The text, without getting too horribly graphic, described a variety of terrors perpetrated during times of constantly recurring conflict around the globe. There were references to the holocaust and other acts of genocide. It described numerous evils that had been carried out in the name of various religions. Marcus thought, *Religion should not lead to violence!"*

Then this entry from Scottish poet Robert Burns, who apparently died in 1796, captured Marcus' attention.

Many and sharp the num'rous ills
Inwoven with our frame!
More pointed still we make ourselves
Regret, remorse, and shame!
And man, whose heav'n-erected face

The smiles of love adorn, –

Man's inhumanity to man

Makes countless thousands mourn!

"*Man's inhumanity to man.*" The phrase rolled around and mingled in with Marcus' present mindset. The young thinker finished the chapter, set the book down and subconsciously directed a question out beyond the world he knew, out toward anyone or anything out there that might possibly be able to propose an answer. *Why have people been so cruel to each other so often throughout history?*

In his mind, silence. He waited. No answer came. He considered the possibility that there was no answer. Maybe the world was stuck forever with the endless and needless suffering created by man's inhumanity to man.

He decided to shift gears and repeated his recent mantra. *Study hard. Get the grades. Escape to college. Put a new band together, a new Yearning.* He continued reading for most of an hour, then went to his room and changed into stage clothes. With the sleeves of his fitted black shirt rolled up, he stuffed his secondhand mint green Fender Telecaster into its case and walked out to the driveway. He laid the classic guitar in the backseat and started up his mom's SUV. The band agreed to meet by 6:30 for sound check and a little backroom vocal warm up before the show started at seven. A Thursday night, the dining area would not be full.

No one gave The Yearning a big introduction, but a pleasant smattering of applause echoed throughout the room as they stepped onto the small platform. Their fan base was growing throughout the area.

Hunter, Marcus' childhood friend kicked off the first song with an unusual rhythm on his high hat and bass drum. Hunter's eyes focused on the high hat, while his face spoke of his joy in drumming. Marcus slipped up to the mic with a winning smile and started the lead vocal.

A little later, the crowd hooted and applauded as the band finished a familiar tune Hunter and Marcus composed together. With a generous dose of Hunter's unique sense of humor, the lyrics anonymously told of an older friend who had married young and was already divorced. The percussion, bass, keyboard and mint green Telecaster brought the song to life.

> I was a lonely guy
> Though I truly tried
> I dated far and wide
> I married fourteen brides
> You could say I lost at love
> The stars did not align above
> Sick with a romantic crud
> I'd never be a stud
>
> Then I met Lola Lovitz
> Ever since I've been out in orbitz
> I'm no longer down in the lonely pitz
> Ever since I met Lola Lovitz

Their divorced friend was puzzled but entertained.

When they finished the song, Marcus found himself wondering if he had met his Lola yet. He thought, *It would be great to find my soulmate, but I wouldn't want all that fighting I hear from my parents.*

Paul Paver, Marcus' dad was an over-the-road truck driver. He had become angrier lately because of news reports predicting self-driving automation. The move would surely put loads of truck drivers out of a job. Gloria tried hard to be a peacemaker in their home, but their home was not a peaceful place.

On the twenty-minute return drive from the hotel that night a phrase from another one of Marcus' originals got lodged in his head. "Soften up. Soften up. You know we've been so hardhearted."

He thought about his parents, especially his dad. *He's hard to get along with at times but has his good qualities. It will be good to get away to college.*

Four

Girls! Of course, girls! A college campus, sidewalks, a student union and classrooms. All full of girls. College girls!

The University of California at Davis had accepted Marcus Paver and Hunter Howell. So, they made their escape from their parents' control. They arrived and dreamed of a new band—and of college girls.

The picnic on their second night on campus offered a social environment for new students. So, the grassy area outside the student union building seemed to them an appropriate venue in which to make their initial connections with the opposite sex.

"Hi. I'm Marcus, and this is Hunter."

Following Marcus' overture, the slightly taller, confident-looking girl with the long blondish hair gazed at the boys through icy blue eyes under russet lashes. She did so without unmasking too great a degree of disinterest. Her two equally eye-catching friends looked on with similar indifference.

Marcus asked, "Are you all interested in music? It's not our major, but we had a band at home. We hope to start a new one here on campus. Hunter's a great drummer."

The blue-eyed girl said, "Yeah. Everybody loves music. So you guys had a garage band?"

The boys glanced at each other and silently registered this minor offense. *How could she diminish the growing fame of The Yearning by calling us a garage band? Where has she been?*

"Well," Marcus answered, "we haven't thought of ourselves as a 'garage band' since ninth grade. We've played many of the best venues around Sacramento." As he said it, he reassured himself that his exaggeration wasn't too overboard. "We've also played in Davis a few times."

She asked, "What was the name of your band?"

Both guys unintentionally answered together. "The Yearning!"

"Nope. Sorry. Never heard of you. At least not yet. Maybe you'll be big someday."

"You never know," answered Hunter.

"Goodbye." And the three heavenly collegiate visions turned and sauntered away. The boys didn't miss the smirky looks on the girls' faces, but they enjoyed watching their hips sway away into the crowd anyway. Their first attempt at meeting college girls. It was painfully short. And disparagingly unfruitful.

Hunter quoted the Lola song. "I was a lonely guy, though I had truly tried. . . . Then I met Lola Lovitz."

"I don't think that was her," concluded Marcus.

"Did I hear you guys say you play with The Yearning?" A somewhat older, strikingly good-looking Hispanic student—unfortunately a male student—had just now expressed an interest.

"Yeah," they replied in unison.

"I've heard you guys, but I don't remember where it was." A long enough pause ensued for the boys to wonder what he thought of the band. He finally added, "I was impressed." *Well, of course he was impressed,* they said to themselves, but not out loud, of course. He added, "I play guitar and bass and do a little writing. I'd love to get together sometime." Things were looking up for the two musical romantic geniuses from Folsom.

Their mild euphoria was soon interrupted by the protesters who came parading through the area. "What's this?" Marcus asked, his question not directed toward anyone who would be able to answer it. In his puzzled mind—*Protesters? Here at new student orientation?*

Up to this point, they were peaceful, just carrying signs as they solemnly strode through the gathering of new students on the lawn. Within fifteen minutes or so they apparently chose to take their protest elsewhere, probably another part of campus.

Short as it was, the demonstration disrupted the fun the boys were having in the middle of their second evening at college. The placards the protesters carried made some statements about guns, but neither Marcus, Hunter nor the Hispanic student had been able to decipher exactly what the protesters wanted to say about guns. It was confusing. The boys were not disappointed to see the placards march away and take the protesters with them.

Their minds went back to college girls. Hunter said, "Those three we just met will be our fans someday. I'm sure of it."

But Marcus sent the conversation in a new direction. "Hunter, you said you were considering the backpacking elective. Did you go with that, or did you decide on a more practical option, maybe the Technology of Bowling?"

"Ha ha, Marcus, old friend, bowling may actually be a more technological pursuit than you think, but, yes, I did sign up for Backpacking 101."

Marcus said, "Outstanding!"

"Yes," replied Hunter, "Outstanding in the Sierras! Or better yet, out hiking, eating and sleeping in the Sierras!"

Five

They were delighted to discover the backpacking elective drew in women, not just men. On the first day of class Hunter and Marcus arrived a few minutes early and climbed the stairs to the second-floor room in the building called The ARC. They settled into the simple but comfortable institutional-type chairs.

Hunter looked around, leaned over and whispered to Marcus, "I see there are a few classy lasses in these here classes!" Marcus returned a goofy, condescending grin in the general direction of his friend. He turned back toward the front of the class, but then jerked his head around for a second look. He whispered back to Hunter, "Guess who's here." Hunter returned a puzzled look. "It's the girl who called us a garage band at orientation."

Hunter uttered, "You're kidding," and snuck a peak. There she was with one of her friends.

Marcus winked and whispered, "They must have heard we signed up for this class."

If they were interested in the musicians from Folsom, they didn't show it. Following the lead of the ladies, the budding rock stars feigned their own disinterest in the girls. Later Hunter told Marcus, "A college freshman has to protect his pride when it comes to the pursuit of the opposite sex. But Marcus, think about this. We are up there backpacking.

It's a cold night, so we start a campfire. The women in our class will surely want to snuggle in close with a couple nearly famous musicians to stay warm."

During class they both got excited about hitting the trail with their professor, Dr. Riley Overton along with her husband, Dr. Matt Overton. He was a psychology professor who had this hour free and sat in with his wife when he could. Toward the end of class though, Marcus and Hunter began to have doubts about going into the wild with these two people when Mrs. Overton held up a book she published titled, *Don't Let Them Take It*. It was a defense of public lands, specifically wilderness lands. With book in hand, she proceeded to demonize every segment of American society that had ever suggested that the federal government had become too powerful. She was obviously passionate to the extreme in her beliefs.

She dismissed the class, and the two friends began their walk toward the cafeteria. Campus was quiet except for the clatter of the maintenance crew's mowers in the distance. Hunter said. "I like our teacher, but some of that skirted a little too close to fanatical. And when I say 'skirted,' it's not that I'm thinking of skirts and those who sometimes wear them. But did she hint that people who share her mindset could form armed vigilante gangs? I don't agree with blasting people away because they get caught logging in the wrong part of the forest."

Marcus replied, "She didn't say that exactly, but it wasn't hard to imagine her approving that kind of extremism, if she thought the circumstances justified it."

Hunter added, "What a mixed bag those people are. They have weird ideas about government but a passionate love for nature. This could be an interesting ride, or I could say a crazy hike."

Marcus said, "I'm wondering if Mr. Dr. Overton completely agrees with his wife's agenda or if he just goes along to keep the peace at home."

Two days later he and Hunter were waiting for their second backpacking class to begin when another student introduced himself. "I'm Darren. I could share some information about our professors, if you're interested." The boys looked at him, and he continued in a quiet voice. "Their trail names match their personalities. The professor's husband has acted wild enough often enough in the wilderness that friends dubbed him 'Madman.' Mrs. Overton is known to have a quick temper. Years ago, her hiking partners started calling her 'Raging River,' and it stuck."

Hunter faked a scared face for a moment before he exclaimed, "We better get outa here while we're still alive!" Marcus and Darren just looked at him until he said, "Okay, we'll be brave and stay."

The boys disciplined themselves and kept their grades up. On the musical front, they connected with the bass player they met at student orientation. For their upcoming venture into the rugged mountains to the east, they needed to find tents, backpacks, trail food and more. They purchased some of it and rented the rest from the university.

The interesting and controversial Drs. Madman and Raging River planned a three-day outing during fall break. They chose a 32-mile loop west of Lake Tahoe. The name of this backcountry area gave the boys a slight chill when they first heard it: Desolation Wilderness.

Six

The trailhead started at the chalet parking lot on Echo Lake. The students had a few hours to acclimate to the elevation, so Hunter and Marcus wandered up to the little store and wondered why it was closed.

"Maybe an elevation thing," surmised Hunter.

Marcus replied, "Probably right."

They heard another voice. "That's it." They turned around and found Darren had slipped up behind them. Marcus couldn't help but think Darren Hastings fell short of the stereotypical image of a backcountry hiker. He was moderately chubby and more academic looking than athletic. Marcus guessed the bulge under his jacket to be some sort of small revolver that he had snuck in against school rules.

Marcus asked himself, *Does he think he could kill a charging bear, or is he looking for a backcountry gunfight with a misplaced street fighter.*

Darren brushed his chestnut bangs away from his black framed glasses and began to educate his two classmates on Echo Chalet. "It's open Memorial Day to Labor Day. It's sorta too cold to swim up here the rest of the year. As the good Drs. Overton said, we could wake up this weekend with our tents covered in snow.

"Another subject. I'll keep it to myself, but I can imagine you two trying to snuggle up with two particular knock-out females by the campfires." Both thought they had hidden their interest better than that, and both silently acknowledged Darren's observational skills. They decided they liked him. He seemed smart and knowledgeable on a host of subjects, including current events.

A distant voice interrupted their chatter. Matt Overton, with his well-worn red backpack already strapped on his shoulders, was waving them in. They followed the rough wooden post and rail fence to the edge of the calm lake where the students were congregating. Both Marcus and Hunter felt and looked unsure about this adventure into the unknown. Matt called out, "Ladies and gentlemen, let's discover Desolation Wilderness."

Before they hiked a quarter mile, Darren started complaining. "This is killing me. But I understand it." He breathed in and out before continuing. "Davis is 52 feet above sea level. Echo Lake is 7,500 . . .. That creates oxygen deprivation. This darn backpack isn't helping." The others nodded their agreement.

For a time, the dominant sound was the rhythm of their creaking boots on the rocky path and their labored breathing. They realized they could hear no traffic noise. No engines running. No horns honking. The unique and prevailing serenity of the high-country setting spoke too compellingly to be missed.

Marcus eventually broke the quietness and did so with adequate respect for the tranquility of the moment. "This place is not as desolate as I thought." Half-winded, staggering his words, Marcus continued. "This is just . . . beautiful. Smell those pines! Clear blue sky! . . . The lake looks so cool from up here." Then he posed a question. "Why would anybody name this place . . . Desolation Wilderness?"

Huffing, Darren said, "It used to be called Devil's Basin. . . . Does that make you feel any better?"

Marcus thought, *This guy adds peripheral details to just about every subject.*

"By the way," Darren added, "did you know you're hiking the Pacific Crest Trail . . . the famous PCT, right now?"

Hunter took a breath and answered, "Yep. You must have observed we always paid attention in class. . ... So, we specifically remember one of the doctors . . . telling us we would be on the PCT. . .. It starts in Guatemala and ends in Alaska."

"Close. Mexico to Canada. . . . 2,650 miles." Darren corrected the comic and added, "Thru-hikers do the whole thing. . . . It takes them five or six months."

"Then let's get started!" was Hunter's decision.

At Tamarack Lake they took a break, dropped their packs and collapsed into the sandy soil. They marveled at the environment, which had become strikingly unforgettable. The calm water reflected the mountains. The clean air provided a surprising relief for their lungs and nostrils, which were accustomed to the compromised atmosphere of the cities down below. Their inner souls—realities of which they were mostly unaware—began to experience the first signs of a rejuvenation they didn't know they needed. Up on their feet again, they hefted their packs to their shoulders.

Within a few minutes, Hunter said, "I feel like I've got a sumo wrestler on my back. Could somebody get him off?" He heard a few groans from his fellow hikers.

They passed a couple more captivating lakes, then left the PCT. The Tahoe Rim Trail led to Susie Lake, which was their destination for this first night out. When they arrived, Marcus declared, "That was the hardest ten miles of my life!"

Riley helped the students search for level spots for their tents. The two from Folsom and their new friend discovered a charred rock fire ring and went to search for dry twigs, sticks and logs, which they deposited by the ring. They were figuring out how to set up their tents when Marcus quietly exclaimed, "Whoa, what's this?" A strange-looking couple was approaching them on the trail.

Seven

The couple looked tired and dirty. Marcus correctly assumed they had hiked in on the PCT from the north. They stopped, and the man asked, "Would you people be okay with us spending the night here? We've been planning to camp by this lake." The college students glanced at each other with puzzled looks.

One of them replied, "I don't know. I guess we could check with our teachers."

"That's fine." Riley and Matt's campsite was close enough that she heard the newcomers' request. "You'll find a few more open spots just past our tents."

These new overnight neighbors appeared oddly uncivilized to the members of Backpacking 101. The students still retained most of the cleanliness of town life, something the two newcomers had lost somewhere north of there. The students and the strangers exchanged antithetical aromas as the couple walked through the tribe of students who were busy setting up camp. The couple caught the foreign scents of soap and perfume. The students caught the native odor of hikers saturated in several days' worth of sweat and campfire smoke.

Everyone continued setting up. Backpacking stoves soon sizzled with hot water for freeze-dried meals, cider, hot chocolate. The fledgling campers helped each other get organized for the night.

The girl student with the beautiful blondish hair, which she had pulled back in a ponytail, knelt beside the fire ring. The boys watched as she held a lighted match under the teepee of kindling, which she built with the firewood they gathered.

Darren expressed his displeasure to Hunter and Marcus in a hushed voice. "Are we okay with Blondie taking over our fire ring? That's our wood." The other two whispered, "No!" Feeling appalled, they stood in place and watched the kindling begin to catch and then grow into a four-foot-tall blaze.

As the sun began to set, everyone, including the two strangers, moved in close to the warmth of the crackling fire. Blondie, whose name was Meagan Wilson, surprised Marcus when she looked directly into his face and smiled warmly. Being careful not to seem overly interested, he smiled back.

The disorderly looking male hiker asked, "You people are apparently a group. Where ya from?"

Marcus answered, "U.C. in Davis. This is Backpacking 101. Riley and Matt, I mean, Dr. Overton and Dr. Overton are our teachers." He tipped his head toward them and went on, "They know what they're doing up here. The rest of us are trying to figure it out."

Riley said, "These are smart students. Matt and I feel privileged to spend this time with them." With faces illumined by the brilliant flames, the students briefly shifted their eyes from the dancing colors of the fire ring to their teacher. A few said "thank you" for her rare compliment.

"Mr. Paver, or may I call you Marcus?" She sent a teasing smile his way. "Up here it's fine for you to call us Matt and Riley, or Madman and Raging River, if you prefer." She finished with a slightly wicked mock expression on her ghostly looking, campfire-lit face.

Then she turned to the strangers and asked, "How about you? Do you come from far away?" The female companion spoke, "We live up by Redding. We've been section hiking various portions of the PCT on and off for several years. This time we started up at Donner Pass."

The man added, "We love the PCT. Lake Tahoe was gorgeous today. The breeze died away. The water became like, you might say, blue glass. The reflections of the mountains were spectacular."

Marcus thought, *This wild man and I agree about something. If he loves calm waters, I hope he'll love keeping things peaceful up here tonight.*

The students were fascinated with their first night in the high-altitude forest. It was a darker darkness than they ever experienced in the cities with the constant flood of artificial light. Strange and wild sounds that most could not identify filtered in from the surrounding terrain. Marcus would admit no fear, but he was glad, inexperienced as he was, that he was not spending his first night in Desolation Wilderness alone.

Meagan rose and tossed a few more logs on the fire. She returned to her place beside Marcus in the circle, and her shoulder bumped against his as she settled in. She caught his eyes glance in her direction and then shift quickly back to the fire. He stifled a grin as a tingling feeling lingered in his shoulder. He told himself, *I'd be okay with some more shoulder bumping with this girl.*

The congenial conversation around the campfire continued except for the times they all got quiet and listened to the inaudible but unmistakable voice of nature all around them.

Then the disruption of that congeniality barged in.

Eight

As soon as the words left the mouth of the southbound hiker, Marcus and most of the others knew Riley Overton would react. No, she would overreact. The hiker questioned, "Have you people heard about those crazies who tried to stop the logging just north of here? They went in and chained themselves to several big, old trees, and the loggers had to stop operations just to avoid hurting them. We love the forest but . . ."

"I certainly am aware of what's happening up here." Riley rushed in. "In fact, a former student of ours is one of those you just referred to as a 'crazy.' She's not crazy. We're proud of her passion to keep big business from destroying our natural ecosystems, including Granite Chief Wilderness, which you just mentioned."

"I'm sorry, ma'am," the hiker cut in. "Please don't take it so personal. I'm sure your former student is a fine young person. But people need to be able to make a living. Our federal government has stolen thousands and thousands of jobs from common people. It's way too heavy-handed in all these matters."

"It's people like you"—Mrs. Overton didn't shout, but her voice took on a militant tone—"who support politicians who have no concept of the danger our environment is in. If the future of our country, and our world for that matter, is left in the hands of people like them, or like you, we'll be headed for a dark future you can't even imagine."

The hiker appeared only slightly taken aback by the overspill from Dr. Raging River. Then like a mountain goat threatened on a ridge he simply steadied himself for a verbal scuffle.

Before the hiker jumped in again, Hunter leaned over and whispered in Marcus' ear. "Looks like the river has begun to rage."

The students watched their professor and their not-so-welcome nighttime visitor spar back and forth. Both used statistics and anecdotes to reinforce their positions. Students recognized worn-out, redundant platitudes. They saw the anger that seethed inside both of them begin to rise, while neither listened much to the other.

Marcus witnessed the hiker stroke the handle of the pistol strapped to his right side and then move his hand over to the log on which he was perched. He also noticed Darren's hand rested on the bulge in the jacket that concealed his holster. The light and warmth of the campfire died away, and their first night in the wilderness grew colder and darker.

Meagan lost the smile she had earlier in the evening. She thought, *I've seen too many families and friends torn apart by these never-ending word wars. Couldn't we have gotten through our first night out here without another verbal battle?*

Darren Hastings, Marcus' new friend, wasn't disappointed. He stood firmly in the camp occupied by Mrs. Overton. He was thinking, *Get her, Dr. River!* Darren often imagined himself a fighter in the increasing American culture wars. He was ready to kick some conservative butt. He thought, *I'll just keep quiet tonight. The good doctor can destroy this pitifully uninformed guy.*

To most of the students, the argument seemed to go on forever, but it didn't. The subject changed, but the mood remained bleak. Before long, they began to get up and wander toward their tents. Some spoke briefly and quietly with each other before unzipping their tent doors and climbing in.

Meagan and Marcus were among the few still standing by the fire. She had thought ahead and had drawn water from the lake to douse the glowing embers. She poured, and the fire fizzed. Thick steam ascended in a substantial little cloud and dissipated quickly. She turned with a slightly quizzical face toward Marcus and spoke a "goodnight." It came out sounding unintentionally more like a question than a wish. As she carefully voiced that one word their eyes met and bonded for an extended moment. "Goodnight," he replied, while he did his best to camouflage the puzzled feeling that danced around inside his chest.

Nine

Day two of the first excursion into the wild greeted the tent campers with an early morning chill in the upper 30s. The first rays of sunlight hit the tops of the peaks. Only the first students out of their tents saw the contentious southbound hiker and his companion finish repacking their gear and hit the trail. In defense of Riley, they saw the strangers as the problem last night and thought, *good riddance.*

Steadily, one by one the ruffled, sleepy-eyed students emerged from their varicolored tents into the crisp, cold, but perfectly calm, clean air. The sun inched its way higher in the eastern sky, and correspondingly the warm rays crept slowly down into the camp. The result was an immediate and entirely welcome increase in temperature.

Across Susie Lake the mountains rose up to produce a magical show for these backcountry rookies. The rocky slopes were mostly gray-colored granite faces decorated throughout with white and black speckles, but occasional slices boasted a less common red and reddish-brown granite. Bands of green pines with narrow, light golden trunks lined the clefts below the peaks and ran along the shoreline.

The trees added long, lively streaks of color to this wild work of art. Parts of the display were duplicated on the reflective surface of the water. The shimmering rays of the sun filtered through the intoxicatingly clean air, danced around on the slopes and painted the scene with constantly shifting, wondrous highlights.

Even Hunter, who had a wisecrack for most situations, was awestruck. He silently, even reverently let the grandeur of this incredible vista soak into his soul. He overheard Meagan's friend Piper, who stood nearby, almost under her breath, but with passion in her voice, utter, "Thank You, God!"

Hunter was puzzled by her expression and asked himself, *Why would she say something like that up here? We're not in a church.* But those three words, "Thank You, God," echoed through his cold ears, into his head and into a mindset that had no category in which to file them. Like an inexplicable current, they sent a strange warmth into an inner part of him, a part with which he was basically out of touch. Unable to shake the feeling, he finally admitted that Piper's words fit the moment, even for a jokester like himself.

The group downed a quick breakfast, packed up and hiked ten more miles down the trail to another enchanting backcountry lake. Campfire that night was pleasurable without the interruption of the previous night. Hunter occasionally threw in one of his goofy one-liners. He claimed to have fallen in love on this trip. Everyone waited patiently for his confession.

"It was Susie. Lake Susie. She was so beautiful!" Most everyone chuckled or laughed out loud.

The chilled adventurers all sat as close as they could to the crackling blaze of the mesmerizing fire. Marcus and Meagan landed side by side again on the circle of logs surrounding the flames. The shoulders of the two brushed together a few times during the evening. Those accidental touches grew less accidental. The time came to put out the fire, and these two wilderness explorers said goodnight and took a little longer to say it.

The troop hiked back to the trailhead by Echo Chalet on the third day. They loaded into the two white, but dirt-smudged U.C.-Davis vans and rode out of Desolation Wilderness with a taste of life in the backcountry they would never forget.

Hunter asked Marcus, "Would I be cheating if I said I'm in love with my drums and with backpacking at the same time?"

Ten

Back on campus, Hunter the drummer and Marcus the songwriter found a bass player. Rafael, or Rafa Milagro, the Hispanic student they met the first night on campus, turned out to be gifted and innovative. The three young men sat together in a circle of chairs they had made in the small practice room in the university's fine arts building. Rafa said, "Yeah. My family emigrated from Venezuela to the U.S."

Marcus noted that his English was as good as any Anglo's, but with an appealing hint of Latino accent mixed in. His narrow, lightly bronze-shaded face was encircled by straight black hair and a sketchy black mustache and beard. He told them, "I play bass and guitar. I write songs when I get inspired. They usually come out in English, sometimes Spanish."

Marcus thought, *This could add a spicy flavor to our show.*

Rafa said, "Hey, *chicos*, I have a new song you should hear. It's called, '*Yo Era un Tipo Solitario.*'" Marcus and Hunter shot a puzzled look across the circle of chairs. Rafa started the instrumental intro to the song on his Alvarez acoustic. Just one measure in they both knew it sounded familiar, and by the second measure they knew what it was.

Marcus exclaimed, "Sounds like Lola Lovitz to me!"

Rafa grinned and translated his title. "I Was a Lonely Guy." They all laughed. A musical friendship was growing, as was a new embodiment of The Yearning.

After more teasing and sharing musical dreams, Hunter asked, "Why did your family leave Venezuela?"

Rafa hesitated. A dark aura flickered briefly across his face. He looked down at his feet momentarily, then said, "You could talk with my papa about that. I was born in Florida. Our family had a very bad experience in South America. I understand my dad couldn't stand one of their presidents, Hugo Chavez. Papa puts lots of blame on that man for the way Venezuela became 'infected'—that was his word—with socialism. He says the economy began to spiral downward. He admits there were other factors involved, but if you get to know him, you find out that he has a strong belief in American capitalism.

"He sees the U.S. as 'a strong fortress'—his words again—of free market enterprise. So, back then, he decided that a move up here would be best for the future of our *familia*. So here we are. We haven't gotten to see our family in South America much, but my parents don't regret moving here. Papa's not happy about what's happening in this country with America moving toward—what he calls—Marxist socialism. In his opinion, that's the cancer that messed up Venezuela's economy."

An awkward silence followed Rafa's story. Hunter wanted to lighten things up, but he kept quiet and thoughtful. Marcus felt slightly overwhelmed and opted to move the conversation toward a less complicated topic. "We're sure glad you landed here in Davis, Rafa. With you in it, the new Yearning has a future."

Rafa relaxed, smiled and said, "*Chico, gracias,* and thank you very much. I can tell you this, the music we will make already has me moving inside! And listen, I know a lady, a friend who's *excelente* on keyboards."

Then with a flourish in his voice, he said, "and she has *una voz maravillosa!*, a marvelous voice."

A meeting was arranged. She fit perfectly. So, Amalia Alvarez filled out the sound the boys were looking for. She had connections on campus, and she worked them to get The Yearning invited to play the student union on the last Friday before Christmas break. They had just enough time to practice and study.

"We have a few days off at Thanksgiving." Marcus said, "I know what we need to do." With October almost checked off, the four friends, Hunter, Rafa, Darren and Marcus sat together that afternoon around a table in the student union snacking on fries and shakes.

Marcus said, "Let's go backpacking. The four of us. I know where we can go."

Hunter was first to respond. "Okay! Well, I think okay. I'm not sure. Do I think, 'okay'?" Then he, Darren and Rafa observed the uncertain looks on each other's faces. Darren was thinking, *Another backpacking trip? We just got back from one, and it wasn't easy.*

Everyone was quiet for a minute, as if a pause button had gotten pushed.

Finally, Marcus said. "Think about it, another deep dive into nature. It could have a significance we don't yet understand."

Everyone clammed up again.

Eventually, Darren turned the tide when he said, "Desolation Wilderness was amazing, and it was probably good for the band to do that together."

Rafa and Hunter both nodded their agreement.

Hunter nabbed a quick sip from his drink, set it back down, looked around and stated, "Okay. And I mean it. But how long are you gonna keep us in suspense, Mr. Wilderness? Are you going to tell us at some point where we're going? We need to start planning our wardrobe, you know."

"It's the coast," Marcus replied, "Point Reyes National Seashore, just north of San Francisco. We can spend two nights and walk to Alamere Falls when the tide is down."

Rafa asked, "What about practice?"

Marcus said, "We can spend Tuesday and Wednesday nights on the trail and be back Thanksgiving Day in the afternoon for family stuff. We can practice after that. Our moms will be glad we didn't disappear for the whole break."

Rafa exclaimed with considerable enthusiasm, "We can practice our vocal parts on the beach! I'm in."

Darren added, "We can bask in the Pacific breezes."

"And we can bring our main squeezes!" That was Hunter.

Marcus said, "Hunter, you don't have a main squeeze."

Hunter conjured up a disappointed, gloomy face.

Marcus said, "Let's make this a brothers-from-other-mothers thing. Amalia won't mind missing three days with four smelly guys on a trail. And Hunter, there'll be other times we can bring girlfriends, if we ever have any. One more thing, I'd like to promote Darren from fan to road man."

Darren replied, "I'm moving up in the world." He smiled at Rafa and said, "The brothers have been wooed. Goodbye, civilized world."

Marcus got right on it, reserved the campsites and downloaded a trail map.

Eleven

"Looks educational," Darren commented as they unloaded in front of Point Reyes Visitor Center.

Hunter protested, "No education allowed. We came out here to get away from all things educational."

Marcus said, "Sky Campground is only a few miles, but they aren't easy miles. Madman lectured us about setting up camp before dark."

So, they started trudging up Mt. Wittenberg. And complaining.

"Does this ever get any easier," questioned Darren who carried his own pounds along with the weight in his pack, which again included a pistol. Rafa had one, too.

Marcus asked, "Pistols, you guys? Did you forget that ounces count in backpacking?"

"These are important ounces," Darren answered.

"Might be needed," added Rafa.

"Okay," Marcus conceded, "but, I'm glad they're your pounds, not mine."

Darren called out, "Hey Rafa, I think Marcus chose this super steep path because he wants to kill us. We might need our guns to defend ourselves against Markie."

Marcus responded with a dismissive goofy look.

"Couldn't you have found a level trail anywhere in the world," complained Hunter.

Rafa, who had never been backpacking, added, "Yeah, Markie, I'm not ready to die."

Markie responded with, "It's Marcus, and stop sniveling. It's only two and a half miles."

"And thirteen-hundred feet of incline!" Darren said what the other two were also thinking.

After a difficult hour, Rafa exclaimed, "Look at that!" All had seen the Pacific Ocean often enough, but this high overlook turned the aqua-colored seascape into a spectacular unfolding manifestation of natural splendor that reached past the horizon.

Rafa said, "Markie, you are one awesome dude. You came up with a perfectly beautiful idea about bringing us out here. I shouldn't have labeled you an undercover death squad leader. If you used to be one, you've been transformed, and it only took an hour."

Marcus answered, "Glad you saw the light, Rafie."

Darkness was closing in when they walked into Sky Camp. They unpacked, set up and fired up their tiny propane camp stoves. The freeze-dried beef stew warmed them in more ways than one.

Woodfires were not allowed. So, they zipped up their jackets and gazed upward into the black night sky punctuated with millions of well-placed, dazzling pinpricks of glimmering light. They told each other stories about growing up and about their families. Their yarns added to their brotherly bonding. Marcus thought, *I hope these friendships last the rest of our lives.*

They crawled out of their tents at dawn the next morning, packed up and started on Sky Trail. The sandy path led them through tunnels of weird-shaped Bishop Pines that crowned overhead. They crushed a few leaves from a California Bay Laurel tree and inhaled the spicy scent. They gazed up at the Douglas Firs that stood as tall as 200 feet. After hiking downhill for an hour and a half, they broke for a rest at a spot with a dazzling ocean view.

"A hiker was killed out here." Everyone turned to Darren, who gave his holster a loving pat and then reassured his friends, "Don't worry; it was 15 years ago. We're close to the old Arch Rock lookout. In March 2015 two hikers were standing on the bluff just above the arch. They were taking in the ocean view like we are right here. Without warning, the ground beneath their feet collapsed. The rocks and dirt became a meat grinder that beat them to a pulp on the 70-foot ride down to the beach. One died. The other was badly injured but survived."

The boys were quiet as that unsettling picture sank in. Then Hunter declared, "Two thoughts. First, that was terrible. Hate that. Second, did any of you feel the ground we're standing on fluctuate, like pretty seriously, about a minute ago?" The rest asked themselves, *Did the ground wiggle, or did Hunter make that up?*

Twelve

Hunter spoke up again. "Speaking of untimely deaths, like the one Darren described, what do we think about our sister school, UCLA? It's been a couple months since those people were killed over there."

The other three shook their heads, acknowledging the tragedy.

Hunter went on. "A natural disaster like what happened here is bad, but a manmade one, like UCLA, is worse. Here's what I heard. A student group brought in a speaker. She promoted censorship of people she didn't like. So, her intended "censorees," who happened to be Republicans, decided to protest. Unfortunately, and so sad, things got really uhg-lee. Two students and an outsider got blasted away. Did I get that right?"

Rafa said, "Basically, yes, but don't make it sound like it was the fault of those who organized the protest. The left-wing group brought in a speaker who is known for trying to silence conservative voices. The protests were legit."

As usual Darren rose quickly to the occasion to defend his side. "She opposes extremists who should be silenced. They're dangerous. They get their people riled up. Too many Americans have been killed because of those people."

"Wait a second," protested Rafa. "Those shots were fired by radicalized lefties."

"No one knows who fired the shots," countered Darren. "It was after dark, and the people were all mixed in together. It wasn't like a Civil War battle with blue coats and gray coats lined up on opposite sides of a field."

"Quit it!" demanded Marcus. "We don't have to rehash all of that again. Can't we just make the most of this peaceful place for a change?"

Darren responded, "Sorry. We didn't mean to upset you."

"I'm not upset!" Marcus said, sounding upset as he said it. "I just get tired of listening to all the bickering all the time. You'd think we could get away from that for a while."

No one said anything. A hawk flew over so low they could hear its wings as it flapped itself out of a glide. They watched it disappear over the tops of the trees. Marcus hoisted his pack. The others followed, and they started down the trail again in strained silence.

After a few minutes Darren glanced back at Rafa, "I guess he thinks he can get us to stop pickin' on each other. Do you think he even has a chance?" Recalling the joyful sharing the night before, he tried to appear hopeful, but his face communicated his realistic doubts. Rafa did not respond, and Marcus made no comment.

The quietness didn't last. Before long the conservative versus progressive arguments commenced once more. Marcus tried to block out the sound of their voices by focusing on the descending trail and the diverse genera of trees and the regularly recurring ocean vistas.

After a few more miles, Alamere Falls appeared. Everyone stopped talking and started paying attention to the sounds of the stream cascading over the tall cliff. The ocean waves washing along the sand and the sea breezes all together changed the mood of the hikers as they descended to the beach. All four friends centered once again on the wonders of creation.

Soon Darren began to inform his friends about Alamere Falls. "It's a rare natural occurrence. They call it a 'tidefall.' There are only two along the entire California coastline. It's a waterfall that falls directly into the ocean. I'm glad Markie brought us out here to see it."

They arrived at the falls and shared the experience with a few day-hikers. They took their boots off and waded into the stream below the falls. They chased the incoming waves of the Pacific Ocean out and back in, again and again. Eventually, Marcus said, "Hate to leave this place, but we've gotta find Wildcat Camp."

It turned out to be a short distance off the beach. They set up tents and downed a supper of tuna packets, Ritz crackers and dried fruit and settled in for the night. The blue hues of the sky and ocean melded into a blend of oranges, yellows and grays on the horizon and then transitioned into darkness. Millions of stars filled the sky. They all felt small and insignificant. The wonders of the environment drew them into a unifying peace that overcame the residue of tension that had been stirred up by Darren and Rafa's quarreling.

Thanksgiving Day began with the chilly air that heralds the sunrise. The four friends wolfed down their granola, coffee and Pop-Tarts and started their grateful march back to the families and turkey dinners that awaited them. They were quiet at first, and Marcus was thinking, *I hope Darren and Rafa don't start arguing again.*

As they rambled through a lush level patch, Hunter began to describe his developing dream. "We've gotten out in the wild together twice this fall. This is good for us, and we make a slick crew, especially since Rafa has gotten onboard. Let's initiate a pact and go somewhere wild in the world at least once a year, every year, until we're ninety years old. Maybe a hundred!"

Marcus hooted like an owl. Then they all hooted.

It was a new bonding ritual that started the night before under the stars. After a couple hours of telling stories and laughing together, a lull occurred in the conversation. During that quiet gap, an owl hooted from out in the darkness. In a hushed voice Darren said, "That was a Northern Spotted owl. I read that they live up here." Hunter tried to imitate the owl. Then they all tried hooting like the owl. Hunter formed big owl-like circles around his eyes with his fingers and hooted again. They all hooted with laughter, and Hunter said, "We owls, we always stick together, now and forever."

Between turkey-time and tinsel-time they studied hard and worked on music. Apparently, the band had garnered enough fame to nearly fill the student union the last Friday night before Christmas break. Many had heard of The Yearning, and others needed a break from cramming for finals. However it happened, the reformed band's first engagement was an Indie folk rock success. Marcus, Hunter, Rafa and Amalia were ready and drew the pleased college crowd into the aura of their sound and style. They grew in renown that night.

Meagan and her Backpacking 101 friend were there. Meagan admitted to Piper, "I kinda like Marcus. He's talented, that's for sure. And cute! We kind of, well, brushed up against each other up in Desolation Wilderness."

Piper said, "I noticed."

Megan went on, "He's kinda quiet and maybe a little full of himself at times, but I think there's more depth to his personality than I saw at first. I guess I shouldn't have called them a garage band when we first met."

Piper chuckled and teased her friend. "Do you think you two might be brushing up against each other again in the near future?" Meagan smiled and winked. Piper playfully brushed her shoulder against Meagan's, and they both laughed.

Along with the crowd, the girls enjoyed the band's creative covers of a mix of the revered tunes of the day. They were also impressed with the enticing plate of originals the band offered up. Before one of the songs, Marcus announced, "The next one is, 'Hey Beautiful Day.'" Applause rippled through the room. "Hunter and I collaborated on it, and we like it. Hope you do, too."

Most of the crowd tuned in to the unique rhythm and the message.

Hey, beautiful day
We like the way you're made
With sunny skies or pouring rain
Happy feelings or a touch of pain
Hey, beautiful day
We think you're custom-made
To move us on our way
Through black and white
Or maybe gray
You help us see
What our eyes rarely see
You help us be
What we can rise to be

Thirteen

Like Meagan, Piper Long also dropped the disinterested act. So, the unusual privilege of getting acquainted with the more serious side of Hunter fell to her. He invited her for a Sunday afternoon walk along the tree-lined, arboretum trail that hugs both banks of Putah Creek on the edge of campus.

With the gentle, flowing sound of the water in the background, Hunter, in his own way, took their conversation deeper than they had gone before. "I'm wondering about something. Remember that *breath-taking* sunrise up in the mountains? Just thinking about it, I. Can't. Breathe! It was 'breathtaking.' Get it? Kidding, as usual, but I'll quit."

Piper smiled.

Hunter plunged in. "You wouldn't know this, but up there I overheard you talk to God. I think that's what you did. Is that what you did? Several of us were up at dawn, out in the cold. We were awestruck, struck with awe, you know. But seriously, I'm trying to be serious. I was close enough to you to hear you whisper. You said, 'Thank You, God.' The way you said those words seemed to fit the occasion perfectly. Here five or six months later I haven't forgotten it."

"It was an unforgettable sunrise," she replied with a look that suggested she still had a clear image in her head. "The big argument around the fire that first night was scary. It's hard to guess where the political ruckus might blow up these days. That next morning the loveliness of the sunrise was such a contrast to the fuss the night before. It was reassuring and gave me a ray of hope for our stressed-out little world."

Piper paused, thoughtful. Hunter waited. Then she said, "I did talk to God up there. And that's not unusual for me."

"Oh yeah?" Hunter replied.

She couldn't tell if his tone was slightly condescending or if he was truly interested. She continued in her quiet, confident way. "I believe in God." She shrugged her shoulders and tilted her head briefly to the side, then added, "I believe God hears my prayers. I think God created that sunrise . . . and every sunrise. God speaks in so many ways, including nature. And how about you, Hunter? What do you believe, basically, about God and about life?"

He was slow to speak. The way he twisted his mouth into a hesitant, quizzical grimace confirmed an assumption Piper had. Hunter was not at all sure what he believed about life and God and religion and all that. Piper waited patiently, her face naturally unpretentious, expressing true kindness and respect.

"Well, I really just don't know much," he finally admitted. "I think . . . I could learn. Maybe I could. You see, nobody in my family has ever gone to church, except for a funeral or to vote—an old church near us was a polling place. Not my parents, not my grandparents. I don't know how far back you'd have to go. There was a time in American history when most people went to church. So, it's probably back there somewhere in my family. I just don't know."

"That's okay." She turned her head and smiled so charmingly that it drew Hunter in like a magnet. He thought, *Wow, what a pretty face! She's so genuine and honest.*

She turned her eyes back to the path as it wove through the pleasant green ambiance of spring and began to chronicle a part of her spiritual story. "I'm the exception in my family. In fifth grade I decided I wanted to go to church. I'm not sure why I even thought of that. I walked to a small worship center a few blocks from us. I didn't understand everything, but I guess I had a thirst to know about God."

Hunter said, "I've never had an experience like that."

Piper said, "Maybe you will."

He said, "Maybe."

Piper explained, "It became hard for me to even think there could be a world with no God. I couldn't swallow the idea that beautiful places, like the Sierras, are accidental."

Hunter quietly gazed over at her face and took in her animated expressions.

She said, "It was natural for me to say what I was thinking that morning in the mountains, even if it came out in a whisper."

Hunter responded, "It was beautiful. But I'm thinking we didn't learn that in school. That's for sure. Quite the opposite. We learned the Big Bang. Evolution. All purely accidental."

"I know," she said, "but that's so hard to believe. Out of nothing and for absolutely no reason at all, the world just started to exist. Then it proceeded from that impossible beginning to evolve into what it is today."

Hunter saw how she contorted her face when she finished that last sentence. He responded, "I think you think that idea needs to be dismissed entirely and immediately."

She answered, "That's a great idea," and continued to explain herself. "Somebody said, 'I don't have enough faith to be an atheist.' I'm like that. Sure, evolution plays a part, to some degree, but it had to start somewhere. God the Creator makes so much more sense to me than something out of nothing for no reason."

Hunter responded, "I see your point, and tell me more, because I'm serious. I hope you have enough faith to believe I can be serious."

"I believe you can be serious when you want to be, Hunter."

"Good, because I'm serious like a final exam when I say there's something about you. And I'm not saying this to weasel my way into being your boyfriend, which I surely wouldn't deserve. But I think you're beautiful on the outside and the inside too."

She smiled kind of bashfully and said, "Thank you! That's so thoughtful of you to say that."

Hunter went on. "I guess you would probably say that some portion of your appealing personality comes directly from God. Right? Forgive me if I'm putting words in your mouth."

Just then two students jogged by together, one male and the other female. Her hair, tied back in a ponytail, swung back and forth with her stride enough to reveal the bold white lettering on the back of her silky black tee-shirt. With uncanny timing it read, "In the beginning God... DEBATE OVER."

Hunter and Piper looked at each other with a "how-could-that-have-just-happened" amazed look on both faces. Not out loud this time, not even a whisper, but Piper spoke the words within herself, "Thank You, God!"

Fourteen

"Hunter Howell, would you come to a gathering with me? You could think of it as a "thank You, God" get together."

He smiled and made a Hunter type face, thinking before answering. *Not surprising she's asking me to come. God is so important to her. I guess God should be important. I hope they don't make me feel guilty for not being religious. Piper never does that.*

He spoke, hesitatingly at first, "Yeah, I think I can come." Then Hunter relaxed and talked more like Hunter. "If I did come, what would I wear? It's way past Christmas, but I could dress up like 'the little drummer boy,' pa-rum pum pum pum?"

Piper was quick. "You could play your drum for Him. Wouldn't that be fun, fun, fun?"

"Ms. Piper Long, you make life more fun. Such an enticing invitation! How could a drummer boy say no?"

They sat close to each other on the cozy couch in the living room of the couple that hosted the gathering. Hunter guessed them to be mid-thirties. After the wife led a study of a passage somewhere in the Bible, Hunter and Piper snacked on chips and salsa and chatted with the mostly twenty-somethings in the dining room.

As they drove away in Piper's car, Hunter said, "I liked the discussion part. It sounds like these God people have struggles in their lives, too, like me. I didn't feel out of place. Besides that, I loved sitting on the couch, right next to you."

He imagined she purred gently as she began her reply. "Mmm, I liked that part, too." A thought went through her mind. *There's a spiritual side to this relationship, but I sure can't deny the attraction I feel.* Hunter wondered, *Am I here because of God, or is it all about Piper?* She prayed, "Lord, help me with this."

Near the end of April with semester's end in sight, Piper accepted Hunter's invitation to go for a walk. "How about the old arboretum trail? We share some history together out there."

She answered, "We do!"

As they began their stroll, Piper said, "It's a wonderful night."

Hunter repeated, "Wonderful night!" and asked, "Have you ever heard of Eric Clapton,"

She replied, "No."

"Classic rock and blues guitar giant from way back. Like yesterday I heard this old tune of his called, 'Wonderful Tonight.' It wasn't about the weather. It was about his girlfriend. I thought of it because my girl-friend looks 'wonderful tonight.'"

Piper soaked in Hunter's charming compliment and returned it with, "And my boyfriend looks wonderful tonight."

They walked hand in hand, and soon that familiar break in the foli-age appeared. The small hidden archway on the side of the trail wooed them toward itself. They slipped through the leafy opening and followed the faint path. An enchanting full moon graced the eastern horizon. Its rays filtered through the branches of the trees and illumined the path. They had never been interrupted back here. They claimed this little sanctuary encircled with trees as their own. They had lost count of the afternoons they had carried a picnic lunch, sat on the grass and shared life.

"What shall we talk about?" she asked when they arrived at their spot.

"We can talk about anything we happen to think about," he responded.

"Well, I can't think of anything. How about you?"

Hunter answered, "No, not really."

"That's okay." Piper was naturally patient and trusted her man to propose an interesting topic. Or he might spin the moment into yet another good laugh.

But this time Hunter notched up his boldness, stepped out on a proverbial limb and stated the following. "I . . . well, I'd like to let our lips"— a short, awkward hesitation—"that is, your lips and mine, do the talking. It's just that you . . . your whole face . . . well, you look wonderful tonight."

"Hunter, you crazy guy!" Piper laughed and smiled and offered him her lovely face and willing lips.

When their mouths parted, they held each other in a lingering moment of close, comfortable quietness. Then Piper breathlessly whispered, "That was magical."

Neither could say how long their kissing lasted in that sweet spot beneath the nearly full moon that unforgettable evening. Even though they were swept away, they exercised a restraint that did not come easy.

After more kissing, hugging, talking, sharing and falling unimaginably in love, they said goodnight in front of her dorm. Hunter had no goofy comment. He did indulge in another quick peck on Piper's welcoming lips, which turned into four or five pecks that weren't all that quick. Finally, he took off inwardly skipping and soaring inside like an eagle on his way back to the apartment he shared with Marcus.

"Our first kiss! Just a little while ago." He knew he could trust Marcus with the news.

"Hunter! First kiss! It's easy to see that it was . . ." Hunter finished his friend's sentence. "Magical. Piper even said it was."

"Good sign! But I'm not surprised. You two . . . there's obviously something . . . magical going on. I can't say I understand the religious side of it, but you both seem so happy together."

Hunter answered, "The religious side. I'm not thinkin' 'bout that part right now. Ya know?"

Marcus replied, "I do" and continued. "Maybe you'll get an 'I do' from her one day in the future."

Hunter answered, "Well, if it ever gets that far. . . . Who knows?"

Smiles all around. Hunter returned to his comedic self and added, "You remember that I fell in love up in Desolation Wilderness." Puzzled look from Marcus. Hunter, with a glassy look in his eye said, "Susie Lake. Remember? I fell in love with Lake Susie; she was so beautiful. Aww. But I swear, it was nothing. I have completely forgotten her. Or 'it.' I guess a lake is just an 'it.' Piper is . . . well, you know. She's a woman! Multidimensional, totally sensational, down-to-earth, of inestimable worth. Wow! What a lady!"

Marcus replied, "multidimensional, sensational, all that! Are you going to come up with a new song for us?" Marcus grinned, so happy for his friend, and delighted for Piper that she had a future with a man as goodhearted as Hunter.

Fifteen

Their freshman year ended, and so did their sophomore year. Hunter and Piper continued to fall in love. Meagan and Marcus were seeing each other but were slow to dive in as deep as their good friends.

At the end of the summer the boys went wilder than ever. They drove up to Yosemite, pitched their tents in Tuolumne Meadows and built a raucous campfire. And one more verbal scuffle started.

"Rafa, what's that organization you joined?" Darren wanted to know.

"What are you talking about?" Rafa responded.

Darren said, "I'm worried about you and that extreme group you're flirting with."

"You probably mean The Solid Society," replied Rafa. "I haven't joined. I've attended a few meetings. It's a solid group, just like the name says. They don't like socialism."

Darren responded in a harsh tone. "Why do you always criticize socialism? The government needs to provide *social* programs that the private sector can't handle efficiently."

Rafa answered, "You think our federal government does anything efficiently. That's a stretch."

Darren said, "Government has its shortcomings, but you're in favor of strong policing. Police protection is a social program."

Rafa shot back, "We need strong policing, but the federal government has taken over so many other aspects of American life that could be handled a million times better by private business, and you know it."

Darren, quietly but sternly said, "I'm just telling you to be careful, Rafa."

Marcus could sense that it was becoming difficult for either of them to affirm friendship with anyone outside their own tribes. He got their attention and asked a simple question. "Can't we try to get along?" No one responded.

As happens, the fire died out and the night grew cold.

The next few days they hiked through Lyell Canyon, up to Vogelsang High Sierra Camp and then struggled through the oxygen deprived air above 10,000 feet on their way to Emeric Lake. They arrived and found the small camping area already inhabited by a lone figure. They visited with him briefly before he excused himself, wandered down the trail and disappeared behind some huge boulders.

Hunter admitted, "That guy makes me feel jittery. Reminds me of that hiker who fought with Dr. Raging River in Desolation Wilderness. This one seems even nuttier." The others agreed.

As dark approached, they started their campfire, and the scraggly stranger invited himself into the circle. The eerie outline of his physical form in the darkness included the contour of a firearm on his left hip. He quietly, solemnly listened to the chatter of the college boys for a while. Then he spoke up with a backwoods inflection in his raspy voice.

"Mountains are my home. I love it up here. So peaceable and pure, unspoiled by all the pollution down there. And too many people. Too many of 'em are pollutin' our nation. They don't really belong here. I need to go back down and get involved. Don't want to, but I can't stand to watch the socialist takeover so many liberal lefties are promotin'. If

America's gonna remain a free country, somebody's gonna have to do somethin' about it."

"Hey, friend," inserted Rafa, "you sound like folks I know who have joined up with—what's the name—Freedom Lost. I think that's it."

"I know of 'em," he responded, "I'm not much of a joiner. I just wanna see major changes in this country, beginning with the way we're being overrun by foreigners, 'specially those invadin' us from the south."

Without even looking, the other three could sense Darren's temperature rising. In a noticeably agitated tone, he blurted out, "You're crazy. You want the big fence. You wanna close up our country to everybody except people who look like you. You would surely send our friend Rafa back to South America if you had half the chance. Your extreme ideas aren't good for anybody."

"Come on, Darren," said Marcus, "give the guy a break."

"He doesn't give Mexicans a break, or Venezuelans for that matter," countered Darren.

It was impossible to miss the outsider getting stirred up. He barked out, "What are you, some kind of radical leftie? It's people like you who are ruinin' this country!" Darren, like the proverbial mountain goat threatened on a ledge, steadied himself for battle.

From that point the two of them rehearsed the well-worn accusations against the two political polarities that had deepened to a seeming point of no return in America and around the globe. The argument continued to boil, and the deep-seated, tribal anger in both kept building.

Rafa said nothing, but he thought, *I appreciate Darren's defense of immigrants, but my family followed the legal process, and we have mixed feelings about those who ignore it.*

Hunter tried to think of a humorous interjection that might redirect this risky exchange, but the battle was too far joined for that to work.

Marcus deeply wished he knew how to mediate between angry fighters. All three of them hoped that this fight would taper off, but it didn't.

Then abruptly all but Darren inwardly gasped as the stranger lifted his pistol out of its holster with his left hand. Darren responded quickly by drawing his. Marcus inwardly exclaimed, *No! No! We don't want this up here!* His memory reverberated with the sounds of shots fired on the street next to the playground when he was in fourth grade.

At this point the stranger's gun was aimed down toward the burning campfire as he sat steadily on his log beside the fire. Darren rested his weapon on his knee with the barrel pointed out into the trees.

Tense. Silence. Nerves. What next?

The fire crackled. A light breeze caused a swaying way up in the trees. The forest tried to speak to these worried men of its longing for goodwill. The stars, with their otherworldly light, endeavored to stir in them a desire for peace among men.

And Marcus Paver stood up. Slowly, intentionally, purposefully, he rose up from his log next to the fire. All eyes shifted briefly toward his dim form with the glow of the campfire highlighting the outlines of his worried but determined face. He took a long, courageous step forward, toward the burning fire, not directly in between the two loaded pistols, but a step closer to that line of potential torrent.

He spoke. "Friends. Friends! Listen. We have more in common than we think."

They heard the hammer of the stranger's pistol cock back. Darren followed suit, ready to defend himself and his friends.

Marcus tried with only minor success to keep his voice from sounding as wobbly as he felt inside. "Men. We are better than this. We don't agree about everything that's happening, not in our country, not around the world, but this is a place of peace. Look at these stars, these trees, this campfire. We have been given so much. Let's not mess it up. Let's not mess up our lives. Let's find a way to fight for what's right without destroying each other. There has to be a way to work together for a better world, not a more violent one."

Darren kept his eyes glued to the stranger, but he listened to Marcus as he continued to speak. Darren also realized a fact he had never understood before. *Marcus is more courageous than I thought.*

Though hard to read, the face of the outsider seemed to register a degree of interest and maybe even a halfhearted consideration of Marcus' words and pleading presence. A few logs in the fire popped and sent an array of sparks flying upward. The pine trees felt as nervous as they do when an out-of-control forest fire approaches. Hunter and Rafa were aware of their own shortness of breath.

Then, surprising himself, Darren decided to follow his friend's lead. Reluctantly, slowly, resolutely, he held the hammer of his pistol back and squeezed the trigger so that he could gently lower the hammer without causing the gun to fire. Through the whole short process, he kept it pointed out into the trees.

The stranger, with a calloused look on his face, continued to hold his gun in his left hand with the barrel pointed down toward the granite circle of stones that contained the campfire. It took a long, breathless minute, but the wild-looking hiker finally lowered his hammer and slid his gun back into its holster. Darren did the same.

Marcus continued to talk. No one remembered exactly what he said. They remembered that he spoke in a calming voice, as calm as he could conceivably conjure up. In a conciliatory manner he expressed respect for the various views held by those in the circle. More importantly, he expressed respect for each person in the circle.

He returned to his place on a log and sat down. He silently asked himself, *Where did that come from? That was beyond me, but it worked. Nobody's shooting any guns.*

They all sat quietly in the forest of fragrant pine trees under a protecting canopy of brilliant stars. Nature's innate tranquility did its best to soothe their agitated emotions.

The rest of the night was not peaceful, not like it should be in the immaculate and majestic high country of Yosemite National Park. All five of them spent a fitful night in their tents. Marcus cocooned himself in his tiny dwelling and quietly fell apart psychologically as he relived those freaky moments by the fire. Darren kept his loaded pistol near his right hand in his little black tent, and the left-handed stranger was gone before daylight.

Sixteen

After Marcus came down from the mountains, he and Meagan spent an evening with his mom and younger sister. His dad was on the road in his 18-wheeler. The two planned to head back to college the next day.

The aromas of pot roast, onions, carrots and spices were drifting in from the kitchen. Marcus put his arm around his mom's shoulder and said, "After a week of granola bars, I'm more than ready for my mom's home cookin'. And I get to share it this with the girl I love. And, unfortunately, my little sister."

Anne made a face and said, "You're fortunate to have me, and you two should get married!"

Big brother responded, "And you should learn to be patient."

She shot back, "You mean patient like Meagan?"

Gloria said, "I'm going to the kitchen, and Anne, you're coming to help me. Come on."

After supper Anne headed downstairs. The rest sat down in the living room to visit. Marcus eventually ventured, "I have a request. Would you two mind listening to a new tune? I always appreciate your feedback."

"Of course!" His mom's response did not surprise him.

Meagan said, "You know I want to hear it."

He grabbed his old Yamaha acoustic from the corner, sat down and shared parts of the developing melody and lyrics.

Where are we?

Where are we going?

Why are we?

Why aren't we slowing?

This conflict, confusion

This hateful infusion

Why can't you hear me?

Or help me hear you?

Meagan assumed easily and correctly that the confrontation up in Yosemite had inspired those lines. Marcus had not told his mom what transpired up there.

"This song is helping you process, isn't it," Meagan suggested.

A short brooding pause followed.

Then, doing her best to avoid sounding too concerned, Gloria said, "Of course, I'm curious about what you're processing." She added, "You don't have to tell me. I'm just curious."

"I guess that first verse gave me away more than I wanted it to," he admitted. "Darren and a stranger got ugly with each other up at Emeric Lake. A political issue, as usual."

"They drew their guns," Meagan blurted out!

"Oh no, Marcus!" Gloria exclaimed.

"They didn't point them at each other," Marcus clarified with the intent to downplay the danger.

"But they drew their guns!" both women exclaimed as they envisioned that disturbing scene.

"What happened?" asked Gloria.

"They argued, and one thing led to another."

"How did it end?"

"No shots fired."

"And...?"

"I kind of talked them down."

Marcus was quiet, lost in thought.

Then he asked, "Does the world really need to be like this? Do people have to get angry and point guns at each other? Seems like we divide into tribes and just let the hate grow. We don't even try to understand or listen to each other."

Meagan let his words hang in the troubled air for a minute. The ceiling fan hummed. Ark the family Beagle angled by and rubbed his spotted side against Marcus' shin.

Then with compassion Meagan spoke clearly. "Keep working with this song. It has potential, and you know better than all of us how music helps us process the wrestling we feel inside."

She brushed her long, multi-toned blonde hair to the side, then thoughtfully went deeper. "It's a struggle more of us should dig into. We accept the violence around us as if . . . as if it's normal. How can the world ever get better if people keep thinking this violence is normal? It's not, or at least it shouldn't be. Common people shouldn't be pointing guns at each other.

"What were the words, Marcus? 'Conflict. Confusion. Infusion. Hateful. Why can't we hear each other?' Was that it?"

Marcus sat sullenly picking at his guitar strings. His two tender companions listened to his disorganized strumming and tried to be hopeful. Eventually, Marcus spoke up, "I sure love both of you. My life would be so much harder if I didn't have my mom and my Meagan. You two are the best."

"I've got a start here. It might work." Marcus spoke with the band when they got back together at school. "People who just want party music won't like it. But some people want a voice crying in the wilderness. That could be us."

Rafa said, "Yeah, man, it's a wasteland out there. Our generation lives in a world falling apart. The Yearning needs to learn to speak with a prophetic voice."

Marcus shared the song.

> Friendships torn
> Mothers mourn
> Streets go red
> Mercy's dead
> Conflict, confusion
> Everyone's losin'
> Can you hear me
> I wanna hear you

The band members all worked their instrumental and vocal magic with their writer's words. When it was ready, they posted a decent recording on social media, and within a week it had gotten more than four thousand listens. Comments included, "We want to hear YOU! Thank you for hearing us." And, "Once more The Yearning has expressed my yearning."

"Professor."

"Yes, sir."

"A member of this class has impacted popular culture this week."

It was a quiet October afternoon at U.C.-Davis. About twenty students sat in comfortable chairs in the artsy "Sociology of Popular Culture" classroom. Class members began to perk up as the same student added, "It's happening right now. Marcus here and his band, The Yearning, recently put out a tune titled, 'Hear Me Hear You.' People are listening. The song has a message about the Trouble."

The timing was in sync with the professor's flexible class plan for the day. He said, "Let's hear it then. Bring it up." In less than a minute the music poured through the class's cutting-edge sound system and filled the room. "Why aren't we slowing? Conflict confusion. Hateful infusion." The last notes sounded, and the prof said, "Play it again. Let's let these lyrics sink in."

After the second play he complimented Marcus, "You've got a gift. Keep it up." Then he moved on to lead the class of mostly junior students into a discussion about the lyrical content of the song. "What theories might explain why we have so much trouble hearing one another today?"

Marcus thought that none of the ideas expressed were headed toward any workable solutions. Most of the students simply blamed their favorite nemeses from the other side for the Trouble. Marcus grew even more skeptical. The words of his song echoed in his head.

> Hear me
> Don't fear me
> See through the smokescreen
> You're not mean
> Reach out

With your heart

Hear me. Hear you. Hear me

Truth can heal you. Heal me

"Hey, you Yearnings!" Darren was first to see the post on the band's page. So, he got to announce, "This is from a music production group in San Francisco, Dark Valley Productions. Here's what they said. 'Heard your song. "Hear Me Hear You." Like it. Let's hear more. Let's talk.'"

The October sun shone through the windows and illuminated the pleasantly surprised faces around the table in the student union. Hunter stayed seated but acted out a dance move with his hands while he said, "Whoa! Ho! Ho! Here we go! Let's go down. We're goin' uptown!" Their surprised faces turned to smiles.

Amalia, the band's keyboardist was there. "It's magic. Where could this be headed?"

Marcus reminded them that this wasn't their first contact from a studio, and the others had dead ended. They wanted more money upfront than students can come up with.

Marcus said, "Let's not hold our breath," which proved to be a wise choice.

Seventeen

Hunter let everyone know he had an announcement to make. They sat together on benches surrounded by colorful, sweet-smelling flowers in the campus garden area. "I'm not sure, but this might leave some of us flabbergasted or maybe dumbstruck." He paused, then continued, "I'm getting . . . are you ready? . . . baptized."

Darren exclaimed, "*Whaaaat?*"

Amalia recovered quicker than the others and enunciated everyone's question. "You're getting what?"

"Baptized, and I expect you to be there—that is, if you want to. It will be cool. Maybe cold. It's March, you know. My teeth might chatter to the extent that I won't be able to say, 'I do.'"

What makes you wanna do that?" she asked with a puzzled look.

Hunter said, "My friends might suggest I'm doing it just to get an 'I do' from Piper when the day comes. I hope I do, but this is not that. I'm doing it because I think it's real. I mean, I know it's real."

"Whadda ya mean, 'it's real?'" Amalia asked.

"Well," Hunter said, "what it means. What it stands for. The, I guess, rightness of it. And what it means for me, now."

"What does it mean for you?" she asked.

Hunter could see the bandmates were fully tuned in. They looked curious as if they couldn't wait to hear the reasoning he would lay out to satisfy Amalia's question. "Basically, I'm getting baptized because I believe in Jesus. Pretty simple, I know. It's not complicated. You all know that a solid drumbeat can lay down a foundation for a song. I'm learning that faith in Jesus is like a foundation for my life.

"I suppose that sounded somewhat un-Hunter-like, so serious and all. But it's really been life-changing for me. I guess you've noticed that I'm a little different, well, more different than I'm always different. Piper has played a big role in this, but it goes beyond her. I think I'll love Piper and worship Jesus and not the other way around." He paused then asked, "Make sense at all?" He scrunched up his mouth and forehead to make a humble, quizzical, uniquely Hunter face.

Darren, who always had something to say about everything, immediately went offensive. "Okay, but don't be one of those 'Jesus is the only way' freaks. Those people will have you condemning everybody to that hot place, if they don't think just like you."

Hunter, knowing that Darren could easily become caustic, wasn't surprised by his critical remark. So, he decided not to respond. In a recent "Thank You, God" get-together, he learned Jesus didn't respond to His accusers when He was arrested, and Peter said not to retaliate when insulted. The cliché, "Turn the other cheek" came from Jesus Himself. So, Hunter sat silently and imagined a slight burning sensation, as if one of his cheeks had been slapped.

Marcus gave Darren a disappointed look and then said to Hunter, "I'll be there. I won't say that I understand it, but you and I go back to the school playground together. That's a long time. I'll be there for you, for sure."

"Thanks," Hunter said.

Rafa added, "My family was Catholic, but they became Christian before they left Venezuela." That statement drew a few puzzled looks.

He went on, "I know Catholics are Christians, but not in Venezuela. They don't think they are. But we got away from church when we came up here. Anyway, I'm coming."

The day came, and they were all there, gathered in the backyard of the couple that led the "Thank You" small group. The yard was graced with a beautifully sculpted in-ground pool. The calm water sparkled blue, looking a bit chilly, but still peaceful and inviting. Newly blossoming lilac bushes added a sweet aroma. As Hunter had predicted, it was not a warm day.

He introduced everyone, including Rosie. "She plays for our small group, and she brought her guitar."

After Rosie led a couple songs unknown to the band, Amalia whispered to Rafa, "That last tune was lovely."

Rosie set her guitar down, and a girl who looked about sixteen stood and spoke the words of a prayer. She didn't read it; she just said it. Hunter's friends caught the emotion in her voice and wondered why she got emotional reciting a prayer. Amalia was thinking, *Did she memorize that or just think it up?*

A normal-looking, middle-aged man, who didn't look at all like a priest, took over. He said, "I'd like to take a minute to explain why a goofy guy like Hunter would get baptized." Hunter smiled. The band members listened intently as the guy talked about faith in God and forgiveness of sins.

When he finished, he motioned to Hunter. Together they stepped down into the water. He asked a question, and Hunter, without shivering at all, responded with complete confidence.

"Do you believe in Jesus Christ as your personal Savior and Lord?"

"I do."

Deeper into the water they went, and under the water went Hunter. Up he came with an impossible-to-miss joy on his face that imprinted itself on the wondering minds of his friends.

Eighteen

Hunter's joy continued. His friends recognized in him a new peace. Piper, of course, made him smile. They had occasional disagreements. Sometimes he laughed off topics she wanted to discuss. He was disappointed with her occasional lack of playfulness, but the pluses far outweighed the minuses for both of them.

As graduation neared, Hunter told his friends, "I have another announcement. It shouldn't be as big a bombshell as the baptism. Could we meet outside the student center Saturday evening and walk over to Black Bear Diner?"

Everyone came. They ordered sandwiches and soft drinks and flavored their meal with stories, laughter and a touch of melancholy with graduation so close. Hunter and Piper sat side by side at the modest, but comfortable downhome cafe table. When they finished eating, everyone quieted down and started staring at them. The two looked directly into each other's faces, and Hunter said, "Piper, you're looking at me like you wonder what I'm going to say."

She responded, "I'm not wondering what you're going to say. I'm wondering how the words might tumble out of your mouth." Everyone chuckled, and Hunter began his announcement.

"Piper and I are . . . we're going to do something. I know we've got you guessing. Shhh! Just wait. I'll tell you in my own sweet time. . . . We are going to . . . Quiet! Okay, you guessed it. We're getting married." The two leaned in and gave each other a tender squeeze. Everyone around the table applauded.

"As if we were surprised!" One of them said it, and they all voiced their agreement.

The usual questions followed. "When?" "Where?"

"This summer. Not sure where."

Then Rafa declared, "Hey, *amigo* and *hermosa* Piper. How about a wedding in the wilderness?"

"Yeah," Hunter replied and sent a grin and a wink to Piper, who did not cease to glow with contentment. The groom-to-be added, "We could stand on top of a big rock, and Pastor Aaron could hang from a tree. He could make monkey sounds. 'Do you—oo, oo, oo—take this cornball to be your tent camping partner forever?'"

Piper provided the appropriate enthusiastic response. "I do!" Everyone hooted with laughter, and the ladies hooted along with them this time.

Graduation came, and they continued their search for jobs in the areas of their new degrees. Hunter made it, just barely—a long way from summa cum laude—but he managed to land a degree in psychology with plans to work hard toward a master's degree. Marcus finished with a double major in creative writing and business communications and put in applications for work in the music recording industry.

Piper spent the rest of May and June finalizing plans for the wedding with her mom's help. The chosen July morning was lovely. The people gathered in the colorful, flower-lined courtyard of the church in which she was raised in Yuba City. Marcus, of course, served as best man and Meagan as Piper's maid-of-honor. Neither Hunter nor his bandmates had much experience with church. Even so, the unfamiliar readings, prayers and atmosphere deepened their curiosity about Hunter and Piper's choice to identify themselves as Christians. The newlyweds moved into grad student housing, and both continued their schooling.

Late in September the band was about to begin a practice when Hunter requested a timeout. Darren had joined them that evening and was sitting in a corner studying. Hunter remained seated on his stool surrounded by his growing set of percussion instruments. The others all turned their eyes toward him and waited. He began with one word. "Oops!" He followed up with an apologetic looking half-frown.

"Well?" Darren asked.

Hunter obligingly and dutifully continued. "Guess who's pregnant. Nope, not me. My bride Piper has begun the process of producing a new human being for the world. And for God who made the world. And for the happiness of her man, which would be me." Nothing like this had ever happened within this circle of friends. So, all were thrilled and awestruck at the same time.

Amalia managed to propose a question. "Planned?"

Hunter responded with a drawn out, "Noooo. But we'll trust that there is a plan, a very good plan for this little fellow."

"Or little girl!" insisted Amalia.

"She would have me wrapped around her little finger. Like already," answered the new dad.

Darren, still sitting in the corner, liked to push the limits. "Are you going to let this child make up their own mind about their gender? Or will you force your 'Christian' narrow-minded views on the poor kid?"

Hunter ignored him, as did everyone else, except that Rafa rolled his eyes.

"When will the little powerhouse arrive here in the world, Dad?" asked Amalia.

Hunter said, "We only found out last week. So maybe, um, Darren could do the math." Everyone got quiet. Hunter prodded a little, "Well?"

Darren looked like he started the math in his head, but then said, "I don't know. Sometime next year. And I sure am happy for you and Piper. Forgive me for being insensitive just now."

"Done deal. You are forgiven for being insensitive just now," responded Hunter as he smiled and added, "love you, bud."

"Thank you, Hunter. Love you too. I'm sorry."

Marcus found Meagan later that evening and shared the news, which she already knew because Piper had told her and asked her to keep it a secret. Meagan and Marcus believed their own marriage was somewhere out on the horizon. Marcus, with an apologetic yet hopeful look, said, "Maybe you and I will be in that position someday." Meagan, with patience, smiled and said, "Hope so. It would be nice."

Everyone worked their jobs or continued their studies through the fall and winter. In the spring Piper looked and felt like a mom-to-be with her figure changing and her morning sickness challenging. Yet the glow always returned to her entire being.

One morning in April in the kitchen of their apartment in grad housing the proud dad patted Mama's tummy. Then he bent down and talked to the encased one they now knew to be a girl.

"Love you! Can't wait for you to show yourself. I will have loads of good jokes for you. And don't worry; I will always be around to protect you from all those bad boys who will want to kiss you." Mommy chuckled. They shared a family hug with their little growing person tucked right in between her lovely mom and comical daddy.

"The name! The name. What's her name?" Hunter wondered out loud. "Did you like Journey?"

"Hmm, maybe," said Piper.

"We'll know when the time is right, won't we!" said Hunter.

Piper answered, "That's right. Be careful out there. Love you to the top of Mt. Whitney and back!"

Hunter said, "Love you forever!"

And he walked out the door to his car.

Nineteen

Hunter had submitted a proposal to his field studies professor. As he drove into the city, he mentally reviewed the project, which read as follows.

> My plan is to visit the county courthouse in Sacramento three times. During each visit I will spend two and a half hours interviewing people concerning their feelings about whatever event brought them to the courthouse. I will disclose my findings and conclusions in a ten-page report.

He arrived around 9:00 AM, entered the long white building with windows all around and spent the next couple hours observing a broad spectrum of humanity. All kinds of attire revealed every walk of life, and all kinds of faces failed to hide varying degrees of worry, disgust or arrogance.

His first prospect was a man around his own age who wore a black tattered jacket, a few chains and tattoos. He introduced himself. "I'm Hunter Howell, a graduate student from UC-Davis. I'm wondering if you have a few minutes and would consider helping me with a class project?" The man shot a mean glare at Hunter and turned away.

He approached three more people who ignored him as if he didn't exist.

He got a little further with a woman who looked about fifty, wore an attractive jacket, slacks and too much makeup. "Hi. I'm a grad student at UC-Davis. I'm wondering if you have a minute to talk."

"Whadda ya want?" was her brusque reply.

"I'm working on a class project in psychology."

She interrupted, "Go away. I don't need your d--- help. Go find some other messed up person to practice your psychology on."

Hunter said, "I'm not here thinking I can help anybody. I thought maybe you could help me."

She scowled, "Forget it. Why don't you just go down the hall."

He took her advice and found a guy who looked late twenties who said, "Hey, thanks, man. Wish I could talk, but I'm on my way in to see a judge."

A woman with a round, rosy-cheeked face sat on a bench and nervously shifted positions and occasionally peered down the hallway. Hunter sat down on the same bench a couple feet from her and introduced himself.

"Oh, hi Hunter," she said. "I'd love to talk. I have 45 minutes to kill before my hearing."

Hunter said, "Thanks."

She added, "It's about an eviction notice. If the judge doesn't work a deal with my landlord, I'll be out on the street. Won't be the first time, but I hate it. What'd you say you're studying?"

"Psychology. I'd like to learn how I can help people."

She said, "Maybe you should be a lawyer. I could use one right now. Or maybe a pastor."

Hunter answered, "Well, I do believe in God. My wife Piper helped me discover the Lord. Can I ask if you believe in God?"

She said, "I sure do. God bless your wife for leading you to Jesus. Do you two have kids?"

Hunter smiled and proudly answered, "We have one on the way, our first."

"How wonderful!" she exclaimed.

They kept talking until Hunter thanked her sincerely and excused himself.

As he walked away, she called out, "God bless that sweet baby of yours!"

For the rest of the morning, most ignored him, and some told him more juicy details than he really wanted to hear. Around 11:30 Hunter and the courthouse parted ways with him full to the brim with the psychological troubles of humanity. He walked south a couple blocks to an old favorite, the reopened Holy Slice Pizza Restaurant for a quick lunch.

He stood up to leave and frowned when he noticed his light-colored shirt was now decorated with a splatter of red marinara sauce. He stepped back out onto the street and heard a faint sound like chanting, or maybe it was loosely organized yelling. He was too far away to understand the words, but the sound seemed to be coming from the state capitol, a block to the south. Curious, he decided to scout it out.

Closer, he started hearing voices shouting, "Bash the fascists!" He also heard, "Un-American is what you are!" He concluded they must be using portable sound systems to amplify their accusations.

Hunter thought, *I've been so wrapped up in psychology classes and marriage and getting ready for our baby to come. I'm clueless about the latest controversies.* As he continued walking, the chants grew louder, and the chanters sounded more agitated.

He decided, *I have no reason to get in the middle of this dog fight, but I'll check it out. It might add to my educational experience this fine morning.* So, he took a left on L Street and stopped under the overhang in front of the post office across from the capitol building. He stood there for 15 or 20 minutes, just watching, learning.

Then. A blast. *Bang!* The whole scene was immediately transformed into chaos. The protesters on the capitol lawn and passersby along the sidewalks dove for cover or threw themselves to the grass or the concrete. The initial hollering stopped, and an eerie silence followed. Obviously afraid that there could be more shooting, everyone appeared to remain frozen to the ground. A minute later, they began to lift their heads and look around before they began their crouched over flights in every direction. Sirens sounded from a distance and grew louder until a swarm of emergency vehicles arrived.

Two police officers had been present all morning monitoring the protest but had slipped briefly into an adjacent shop to grab coffees. Before they could order, they heard the single shot and ran out into the chaotic situation. Almost as fast as they reappeared, the protesters began to disappear.

The two officers ran in opposite directions. One stopped and knelt beside an injured person on the sidewalk then stood and waved to the first medical personnel to jump out of an ambulance.

The other searched for eyewitnesses. It took several minutes before he found one who would talk with him, a middle-aged woman who kept sobbing. The officer patiently tried to help her settle down and finally asked, "Ma'am, can you tell me what you saw?" She continued to struggle with her emotions as she pulled out a Kleenex and wiped her eyes.

Then she said with conviction. "Life in this country is not supposed to be like this."

He replied, "That is so true." He gave her a moment, then asked, "What happened out here?"

She took a deep breath and answered, "I was walking . . . from the Hyatt where I work. I'd planned to go down the street for pizza." She wiped tears from her bleary eyes and reddened cheeks again, this time with the yellow plaid sleeve of her shirt. "The protests always make me nervous, but we see so much of it here at the Capitol. I've never gotten used to all this, but I guess you still have to do what you have to do." She looked down and shook her head.

"Yeah, that's true, but can you tell me what you saw? What happened out here this morning?" the officer asked again.

"Well, it was horrible! Several people were standing in front of the post office. I guess they were watching the protest. I was walking toward them. Then a gun went off. *Bam!*" She closed her eyes and used both hands to wipe more tears from her cheeks. She peered at the officer. "From the sound of it, it must have come from over there." She pointed toward the capitol building. "When the gun went off, one of the people standing here fell. There's the blood, right there on the sidewalk."

The woman continued, "I feel so sorry for that person and for their family too, if they have one. The ambulance got here. Quick. They picked the individual up and loaded him in the ambulance. I think it was a male, but I'm not sure. They drove away fast. I hope whoever it was makes it. I will pray for them. I'll never be able to wipe this out of my mind. How can people with their guns be so careless about injuring innocent bystanders?"

"Thank you, Ma'am, for your help. I'm sorry you had to see this. It just isn't right, is it?" The police officer pressed a little further. "Did you see the person who fired the gun?"

She said, "No. I wasn't looking that way. I just heard the *bang* and saw the person fall. And the blood. It was terrible."

He said, "I'm so sorry. I'll need your name and contact information as an eyewitness."

She answered, "Okay. I'm sorry I can't be more help."

Twenty

Piper answered her phone.

"Is this Piper Howell?"

"Yes."

"This is Officer Murkle with the Sacramento Police Department."

Silence.

"Are you there, Mrs. Howell?"

"I'm here. What do you want?" Piper considered this could be a stupid scam.

"Mrs. Howell, I'm down here at Mercy General Hospital here in Sacramento. I'm calling about Hunter Howell. We found your number in his cell phone. Can you tell me what your relationship is to Mr. Howell?"

"Hunter is my husband. What's wrong? Was he in an accident?"

"Well, it was an accident of sorts. We hate it when things like this happen."

"What happened?" Piper's voice erupted in a controlled outburst.

Officer Murkle spoke steadily, "Your husband was downtown by the Capitol a little while ago. Another one of those protests went bad. A stray bullet—"

Piper couldn't hear as the world started to slip out from under her feet. She fought to control the rising hysteria inside her gut.

She heard the strange voice say, "He's alive, but he's in serious condition. Do you have a family member or friend who could drive you over here as soon as possible?"

A tiny, fearful "yes" squeaked out through her throat.

"It's Mercy General in Sacramento. The address is…"

"I know where it is. Oh God, help me!"

She desperately tried to stay calm. She hung up the phone and hung onto the hope that what happened would not be as bad as it seemed. She told herself, *My sweet, goofy Hunter boy will pull through this, whatever it is. He will. I know he will.* She prayed, "Dear God, help us. Maybe it isn't that bad. He'll be okay. I need him! Our baby needs him!" And she massaged her growing abdomen and prayed that God would help this baby's daddy be all right.

Meagan didn't answer her phone, but Rafa did. Piper whispered, "Thank You, God."

"Rafa, this is Piper. I need…" and her muffled voice trailed off.

He immediately knew Piper was not her normal composed self. With a shaky voice, she eked out, "Rafa, something bad has happened to Hunter." Silence, then, "He's in the hospital in Sacramento. Can you come get me and take me there?"

"Hey, Piper, you sound really upset. Is this serious?"

"He got hit. Somebody shot a gun. They hit him. What did he do to deserve this? I don't even know why he was there. He drove over there earlier—can you come get me? Please?"

"I'm coming, Piper. I'm leaving right now."

They parked and ran down the gloomy sidewalk toward the gaping, surgical looking entry into the mouth of a roaring beast. So it seemed to Piper. All surreal. Unfamiliar sounds. White surgical coats and turquoise scrubs. Worried people sat in chairs along cream-colored hallways with occasional patches of color. Others rushed up and down the corridors. They heard beeping sounds from rooms with half-open doors. Two men in light blue scrubs swiftly pushed a bandaged woman on a gurney past them. Nurses sat behind long counters typing or speaking into their computers. Others stood there as if nothing was wrong with the world.

Rafa was confused and overwhelmed, but grateful to be the one to support his friend's bride, this new mom-to-be. He traveled close beside her in a ghastly slow-motion climb up a mountain that was surely too hard to climb. Mixed in with his compassion for her was his own broken feeling and fear concerning a friend who had welcomed him, made him laugh, and had brightened his whole life. *Oh God,* he exclaimed within himself to a God he wasn't sure existed.

They found him in ICU. The scene inflicted a sick feeling on Piper and Rafa. The weird sounds of the ventilator that forced air into poor Hunter's lungs seemed otherworldly to them. There were tubes going everywhere from beeping machines with black screens that displayed blinking red and green numbers and charts. It seemed that every tube in the room had found its way into some part of Hunter's limp body. Piper's stomach suddenly turned so squeamish she visually searched the room for a trashcan. She forced her body to cooperate so she could do what she needed to do. She found her beloved's hand and held it tight.

She prayed. And prayed more. She pleaded. She sobbed but tried to maintain composure for her husband even though he was obviously in another world. "Hunter, please hang on. Get better. We all love you. I love you so much! I'm here." She stopped speaking, overcome with the pain. She closed her eyes, and her head slumped down. She searched for strength. She looked at her wounded husband and spoke again. "I love you. I won't leave you alone. I'm praying to God. 'Please help me and this little girl inside me.' She's your little girl, Hunter. Come on. You can get through this. We can . . . do this."

Hunter's mother arrived. Piper had managed to get a text off to her from Rafa's car on the way from Davis. This adoring mom grew overwhelmingly weak-kneed and ashen-faced when she rushed in and her eyes lighted upon her unconscious, anemic-looking son. Her mind momentarily flashed back to her Hunter boy when he was little. She thought, *He has made everyone laugh over and over throughout his whole life. How could this happen to this happy angel of mine? He has to come through this. His baby needs him. We all need him. Piper needs him.*

Rafa stared at his phone, dreading the call he had to make. *This is going to kill Marcus,* he thought. *These two have been best friends forever.*

"Marcus, this is Rafa."

Marcus answered, "Hey, buddy, great to hear from you. How's your day going?"

"Not good," was the dark toned response that came back.

Marcus sounded uneasy. "What's up?"

Rafa said, "I'm at Mercy General Hospital in Sacramento. With Piper."

Marcus asked, "Did she get hurt somehow? Is the baby okay?"

Rafa said, "It's Hunter."

Silence.

Marcus stared straight ahead, not focusing on anything. He repeated Rafa's answer. "It's Hunter. What happened?"

Rafa told him. "He got shot."

"*What!*" Marcus struggled to let those words sink in. He told Rafa, "I'm coming."

"Meagan, I need you." He had to leave a voicemail. "I'm on my way to Mercy General Hospital. Rafa says Hunter got shot. I can't believe it. How could this happen? I've dreamed about it for years. Nightmares! Please call me."

Marcus arrived and impatiently waited for the elevator, which then moved upward in painful slow motion to the third floor. He darted down the hall into the Intensive Care Unit, past a busy nurses' station, and in through the sliding glass-door. He pushed past the grey dividing curtain into the bizarre little room where he found his long-time best friend unconscious, on a ventilator and surrounded by a crowd of uncaring, beeping machines.

Piper was staring at Hunter's blank face, crying, and holding his hand. Rafa stood in a corner of the room looking bewildered. Hunter's mom sat across the bed from Piper. Between them Hunter lay breathing in and out in sync with the timing of the ventilator. Marcus focused in on the heartbreak in Hunter's mom's face. He turned his eyes and stared at the lifeless looking form in the bed. As he spoke his friend's name, he began to fight back the tears. He looked around the room and found nothing but pain and sorrow. His own breathing came short and shallow.

He eventually got the story, as much as they had all been able to piece it together. Hunter was downtown in Sacramento that morning near the capitol building. Somebody shot him. Marcus asked, *Why? Why! Why would anybody shoot Hunter? He doesn't hurt other people. He's kind. Innocent. Why?*

The doctors who rotated in and out had all been gracious but non-committal. None of them had painted a hopeful picture at all about their comatose patient.

Why Hunter? Marcus wanted to scream those words at the top of his lungs, but he considered his own pain must pale in comparison to what Piper must be experiencing. He wanted to be a comfort to her, but he had no idea what to say.

He left the room later that evening. As he approached the hospital entrance, he fought with his desire to slam his fist against the glass door. In utter frustration he told himself, *I hate them! I've tried so hard to see the good in people. I've tried not to hate, but this is too much. Why do people keep this violence going? It never stops. It's inhumanity all the time. People are disgusting.*

Twenty-One

The story made the local television and online news sources. But the shooting was not the main story of the day, not even in Sacramento. The action of the state legislature inside the capitol building eclipsed the violence outside it. A bill narrowly passed that would outlaw driver-controlled trucking in the state of California by the year 2038.

The big news of the day was not the fact that another protest bystander took a bullet. It was not big news unless you were Piper Howell or the child growing inside her, or Hunter Howell's family or Marcus Paver.

Piper spent the next three days in the dark, lonely, eerie valley of the shadow of death. She hardly ate a thing. Her face grew gaunt with eyes resembling those of an orphaned child in some distant war-torn country. Rafa Milagro thought, *Hunter did not deserve this, and neither did she. What did she ever do to earn a place in a hellhole like this?*

On day three Piper agreed to let them unplug the machines. She felt like her heart was getting unplugged from its life source. Still, she sat faithfully by his hospital bed, holding his lifeless hand. Piper's mom sat with her arm around her broken daughter. Her dad stood stone-faced behind them. Meagan kept her arm around Marcus' shoulder while he struggled to keep his weeping under control. Rafa stood alone in a corner. In less than thirty minutes Hunter was gone.

Medical personnel took him away, and a chaplain led his family and friends to a small, private, waiting room. Before long someone brought a report and handed it to Hunter's mom. She studied it for a few minutes and then steadied herself enough that she was able to share the gist of the report with the others. "Hunter's organs are going every direction. He is giving life to at least a dozen people. In fact, one of his lungs is already flying north to Seattle. The young woman who will receive it is about Hunter's age. She was also an innocent victim of a political skirmish." She stopped and cried. She started again. "Hunter would be glad to know that someone will keep breathing in this world because he gave a part of himself to her."

Everyone was quiet for a couple minutes before Meagan spoke. "Here's what I think. It's too bad they couldn't transplant Hunter's unique sense of humor into some humorless person out there."

Someone in the room said, "Good point!"

Marcus said, "I can think of hundreds of mean-spirited extremists who need an implant of Hunter's gentle personality. The country would immediately improve if everyone was forced to take an infusion of his kindness and humility."

Pastor Aaron, who conducted their wedding less than six months earlier, presided over the groom's "celebration of life." Piper looked broken but mysteriously dignified in her singular-looking black maternity dress. Her tear-streaked face spoke of her pain and her courage. Marcus and Rafa appeared lost. They both noticed that Darren was struggling to keep is anger under control.

The newly widowed young mom-to-be heard little of what was said during the service with one exception. The pastor quoted Psalm 23 in his eulogy. With tender compassion he asked the gathered people if they knew why death has a shadow. "'Yea, though I walk through the valley of the shadow of death, I will fear no evil.' Death has a shadow because there's a light on the other side. A tree casts a shadow because the sun is shining on the opposite side of the tree. Death casts a shadow because the light of Jesus shines from the other side. Young Hunter saw that light and believed in it. His freewill choice to be baptized in the name of Jesus tells us that he truly believed in the light of Jesus."

Piper let the pastor's words assuage her injured psyche to a degree. When the service ended, she graciously received compassionate hugs and loving offers from friends and even strangers to help in any way they could. But she soon began to excuse herself. She turned down offers from her mother and from Meagan to stay with her overnight and told them she needed to be alone.

She let her mother and dad drop her off at her lonely apartment in married student housing. She changed into jeans and a light blue top. She remembered it was a favorite of Hunter's and sobbed again. After her weeping began to subside, she spoke to herself about her future.

At some point I have to pull it together. And rebuild. For this little girl and for myself, too. But not today. Today, I need to keep breathing . . . . "Dear God, help me. I trust You, and I always will. But this is so impossible for me. I can't do it without You."

Marcus woke the day after the funeral with a dream lingering in his half-conscious thoughts. In his dream Piper was waking up in her bed. She reached over to where Hunter should have been, lying there beside her. Instead, she found nothing but cold sheets. She jerked her hand back and cried out.

Falling back on his longtime habit of working through life issues by writing lyrics, Marcus turned the dream about Piper into a song. He spoke the lines into his phone.

Woke up
Reached out
Empty space
Vacant place
No warm aroma hung on
No driving beat played on

No pot percolated
Down the hall
An empty table
A forlorn fable
No kitchen chatter
What does it matter

My world is slipping
My ship is sinking

But I will see you again
I will reach up to you, my absent friend
We will put this pain at bay
O God, help me make it through this day
Somehow, some way, again we'll kiss
O God, help me walk through this

Marcus thought another verse would tell of the baby, nestled inside her mama's womb, safe, unknowing, protected, waiting to be welcomed into what kind of world.

From the day of the shooting and each day after it, Meagan did her best to carry Marcus forward. Together they wept and vented the pain deep inside both of them. They held each other in their arms and sought comfort for themselves, for Piper, Rafa, Darren, Amalia and the rest.

Ironically, Marcus landed a job with the recording company in San Francisco, the same one that contacted The Yearning a couple years earlier, Dark Valley Productions. He was grateful to find work in the music industry but feared his own musical dreams may have died on the street outside the Capitol. The band canceled a bundle of promising bookings while they tried to figure out what to do without Hunter. They felt like they were in the dark even on the sunniest days that summer.

On the twenty-ninth of June phones began to ring or ding. Piper's mom was rushing her to Metro Birthing Center. The staff immediately and compassionately cared for Piper, her pre-born baby and for the wounded hearts they knew Piper and her mom brought with them. As the midwife calmly visited with Piper in between contractions, Piper confided, "I've decided to name her Journey. Hunter liked that name."

Family and friends started arriving and lining their vehicles up beneath the spreading oaks that shaded the small parking lot. Piper's friends, all four of the new grandparents, a brother, and a few cousins all rushed in. The receptionist ushered them into the facility's comfortable waiting room. They filled most of the couches and chairs. No one needed to say how badly they all wished Hunter were there.

They waited and then heard crying down the hall. Before long, a nurse appeared and announced, "We have a baby girl! She is healthy and strong. You probably heard what she could do with those powerful lungs of hers."

Everyone in the waiting room cheered. Piper's mom said, "Her cry is a ray of sunshine in this tearful world. Her daddy would be so proud. I know he is."

A half hour later, Baby Journey's admirers were peering through the glass to see her. They cried, and they tried to describe to each other how beautiful she was. Since it was late, the midwife encouraged Piper to stay overnight, which she did. Her parents picked her up in the morning and took her and the baby to their house in Yuba City where they spent the next few weeks.

Marcus was enamored with Baby Journey, but still broken. By August he knew he needed to escape, if only for a few days. His boss understood. As he crammed the backcountry necessities into his backpack, he spoke to himself. *I need to stuff something else in here, like a little relief from this constant pain.*

Twenty-Two

Wandering through the darkness of his emotions, he drove east into the Sierras. The turnoff to Desolation Wilderness appeared, and he recalled the night Hunter joked about falling in love with Lake Susie. The thought drifted through his mind: *the original fuse between Hunter and Piper was lit up here.* With a deep groan he uttered, *how I loved that guy! Great sense of humor! Talented. Kind. What a senseless, stupid loss! His death sent all of us into a desolate wilderness.*

Up here Piper whispered something about God that affected Hunter so much. I still don't understand why religion became so important to him.

Marcus didn't pray as he drove along. At least, he didn't think of it as prayer. But he talked to God and did so in a way that discarded every semblance of reverence. Above the grumble of the truck's engine his words cried out with unbridled sarcasm.

"Hey, if there's a God up there somewhere, yeah You! Why didn't You help my friend? He said he turned to You. Why didn't You turn to him and his wife and their baby?" *I don't know why he ever believed in God anyway. How could Hunter think that some God up there loved him and then let him die with his blood splattered all over the sidewalk? What kind of loving God is that?*

His anguish continued as he traveled through a dark night on a road that seemed to head toward nothing but more darkness. He crossed the state line into Nevada and turned south on US 395. The road quickly angled back toward Lee Vining, California where state highway 120 turns west into Yosemite. Raging River and Madman had often bragged about the whole majestic east side of the Sierras. Even in his depressed state, Marcus was moved by the magnificent scenery.

In Bishop, beneath the shadow of the massive peaks, Marcus learned about the Eastern Sierra Visitor Center an hour farther south. They provided the needed permits, trail maps and weather and water reports. Marcus climbed back in and drove his old pickup up the steep grade toward Horseshoe Meadows Campground. Halfway up the 6,000 foot incline rain started as a sprinkle but turned into an unusual August downpour. Arriving, he parked by an empty campsite and sat listening for 45 minutes as the rain continued to pound the roof of his truck.

It finally slacked off, and Marcus climbed out of the vehicle. He stood for a couple minutes and watched the rays of the sunset filter through the golden-brown trunks of the trees and illuminate the brightly colored tents farther down the campground. Breaking clouds became red and golden glories in the western sky.

His eyes rested on a diminutive crimson tent huddled among the pines and sage brush a hundred feet away. Despite the rain-soaked conditions, the camper, a lady whistled while she stirred a miniature blackened pot over a bright, well-contained little fire. A light breeze blew an enticing aroma over toward Marcus. He wondered how she was able to start that fire after the deluge had drenched all the kindling. He didn't recognize the tune, but he thought her whistling sounded too cheerful. He thought, *I wish that lady would shut up!*

He wasn't too thrilled when she overtook him the next morning about an hour and a half into the climb up toward Cottonwood Pass. "Hey! How ya doin'?" she asked as her bootsteps caught up with his. He thought, *Go away, and leave me alone*, but grudgingly responded, "Fine."

He tried not to scowl as he thought, *People her age shouldn't be hiking up inclines this steep. She might suffer a heart attack.*

"You like that pack?" she asked in a friendly tone.

"It's fine," Marcus replied in a curt and cold voice he hoped would douse any small blaze of conversation.

She said, "Hey, I hope you have a great trek and find whatever you're lookin' for up here." Then she throttled up the hill and left Marcus feeling slow and outperformed. He thought, *Who cares*, and he directed himself back to the job of lugging his grieving soul, body and backpack up the mountain.

He planted one heavy foot in front of the other for five miles up 1,300 feet of elevation gain. His effort landed him up beside Chicken Spring Lake on the Pacific Crest Trail. The cliffs rise several hundred feet on the east side of the lake. Marcus thought, *Nice. These mountains make a great barricade. The uglies won't be able to climb up here. I can escape all that for a few days.*

The area was by no means crowded, but he was not alone. He filed past six or seven tents. A few campers looked up from their chores and spoke greetings. One tent resembled the one that belonged to that older woman, but he didn't see her. The quiet chatter of the other hikers bumped against his tired ears and made him feel alone. He found a spot a short way back from the edge of the quiet water of the tarn, which he guessed to be a couple hundred yards across.

Dark arrived before long, and Marcus was amazed when someone turned on a bright spotlight. It turned out to be the nearly full moon as it ascended without hesitation over the shadowy cliffs behind the lake. The moonlight cast a calming sensation over him, even though he continued to feel the pain lurking beneath the surface. Worn out from the strenuous climb up from Horseshoe Meadows, combined with the thinner air at 11,000 feet, Marcus collapsed into sleep.

He had no idea how long he slept in his tiny dwelling before he began to revive toward semi-consciousness? Contrasting images from a dream brewed in his head. Hunter was injured and was struggling to breathe. He wanted to live but was lost in deep water and sinking beneath the waves. Then suddenly from somewhere up above a dazzling, nearly blinding light streamed down out of the sky. It speaklessly searched for and found Hunter below the churning whitecaps and drew him up into itself. Hunter's struggle was over. No longer sinking, he was gathered up to a faraway place in the sky. As Marcus became more fully awake, he supposed the dream had something to do with his friend's Christian faith. He felt some comfort in that.

Now mostly awake, he climbed out of his tent to relieve himself. In the still night air, cloaked in his grief, he looked up at the sky with its numberless stars. The moon reflected its light down on him.

In the stillness he heard the voice of Piper, an echo of what Hunter had heard and shared with him. In college on their first backpacking trip, she and Hunter were taking in their first glorious mountain sunrise when Piper whispered three words. Her quiet litany had shined a bright light into Hunter's surprised heart. Now the same short phrase murmured like a brook down through the last few years and flowed into Marcus' lost soul. Though the words still seemed foreign, they had developed a mysterious power. He slipped back into his down bag and thought about those three words. "Thank You, God."

Twenty-Three

Dawn came, and Marcus pulled himself out of his bag into the chilly air of the new day. He decided to postpone breakfast until a stop on the trail. He packed his gear and headed north on a portion of the PCT that wove through fields of granite boulders, some as small as a pebble, others as large as a Volkswagen Bug. Gnarled foxtail pines lined the trail and decorated the meadows in the crisp looking Sierra valleys to the west and north. Marcus followed the trail up and down for a few miles and stopped at the Siberian Pass trail junction. He stripped off his pack, picked out a rock shelf to sit on and began to nibble the breakfast he had stuffed into the top pocket of his backpack.

He had just opened his blueberry Pop-Tarts and stirred Tang into a cup of purified water from the lake when he noticed a hiker approaching from the south. *Oh no,* he realized, *it's that overly friendly old woman. I don't wanna talk with her. Keep going, lady!*

She reached the junction, said "Hello" and took a few steps past Marcus. He felt relief until she stopped and turned around. "Beautiful scenery up here, isn't it?" Marcus took a deep breath and looked away. She added, "And the air is so crisp and clean after that surprising rainstorm. Of course, it's always crisp and clean up here. That's especially true when you compare it to down there, where the cars are, and the exhaust and the noise. Know what I mean?"

"Yeah," Marcus replied and gazed out over the valley again. He nibbled on his Pop-Tart.

She went on. "I don't know about you, but I feel fortunate. I've gotten to spend a pretty good portion of my life outdoors. I was blessed to serve as a park ranger in several of the national parks. I did that for 26 years. I love this."

"Good for you," was Marcus' unexcited and noticeably sarcastic toned response. Yet without saying so, he admitted, *Hmm, park ranger. That's interesting.*

She brushed off the unpleasant sound of his voice and asked, "Are you a guy who has been out in the wild a lot?"

"No," was his blunt reply.

She waited patiently and turned her face west to peer down into the valley that contained Big Whitney Meadow nestled between the surrounding granite mountains. A marmot appeared beside the trunk of a foxtail pine on the slope below them, took a look at Marcus and his visitor and quickly disappeared behind a rock.

Marcus finally spoke in a slightly hospitable but measured manner. "I really just got started in college. Friends and I went out." He stopped and looked down at his boots. Appearing noticeably unhappy he added, "It wasn't all good." A frown fell across his bothered face.

She removed her blue hat, unhooked the straps of her weathered gray pack with its dusty red highlights, wiggled her arms out and leaned her pack against a rock. "Would it be okay if I rested here a little? I need a break."

Marcus took another deep breath, sighed, and said, "Go ahead. It's not my trail."

She sat down on the almost level trunk of an old fallen tree. Marcus thought, *Great! How long am I gonna be stuck with her?*

She told him, "It's good to hit the trails with friends, or without them. I have pals who go with me, but this time I needed to go alone. A lot of hikers use the trail to process their thoughts and worries."

She paused briefly. A thought flitted through Marcus' mind. *She might have troubles she's dealing with. And I'm sorry, but I don't care. I've already got too much emotional baggage of my own to carry up and down these mountains.*

She went on, "Did you decide you wanted to go solo this time, or were your friends all busy?"

He closed his eyes and pressed his lips together. As he turned his face toward his intruder, he remembered his mother teaching him to speak respectfully, even when irritated. "Ma'am. I'm not really. . . I don't know. It's been a tough summer. You seem like a good person, but it's hard for me to talk about . . . you know, it's my life." In his unspoken thoughts he added, *And don't invade my space.*

She responded first with her face with which she effectively communicated compassion. Marcus caught it and thought, *I don't think she's play-acting. She seems concerned, like a mother would be. I guess it's her age.* Though he fought with it, he felt a moistening in his eyes. His desire to remain detached began to melt slowly like the mountain snowpack in early spring. He was surprised by his need to talk. To anybody. To this surrogate motherly figure who sat on a log on the other side of a mountain trail.

He sighed deeply and said, "My friend died. He was killed by a stray bullet outside the Capitol this spring. We were best friends. Since grade school. Why would a good guy like him have to get killed for someone else's stupid political ideas? He hardly cared about politics. So, yeah, I'm up here processing, like you said. I'm trying to make sense of this." He stopped, feeling as lost as ever and asked himself, *Why am I spilling my guts to this stranger?*

She did not speak right away. She did her best to absorb the pain coming from the hurting young man across the path from her. She also told herself that this was not an accidental encounter. She uttered, "Oh, how terrible!" then waited.

A light breeze caused the pine needles above them to perform a leisurely ballet on the branches. The distinct scent of the trees added a soothing touch. And two strangers crossed a border into an unexpected human connection.

"What *is* your friend's name?" she asked. Marcus noticed that she used the present tense to refer to someone who didn't exist anymore. "He *was* Hunter."

"Hunter." She repeated the name. "If you want to, but only if you want to, tell me about Hunter, anything you want to tell me. I'd love to hear. I really would. What kind of person is he?"

Marcus said, "Well, he isn't anymore. He's gone. Dead. He doesn't exist anymore."

She said, "Not at all? Not in any way?"

Marcus answered, "I guess he lives in my memories. But he's dead; he's gone."

The woman said, "Some people believe that we live after we die. Lots of people believe that."

Marcus laid out his sharp and curt reply in a skeptical and unmistakably cynical tone. "I suppose."

She waited and watched as the young man shuffled the fallen, dark golden pine needles that lay beneath his feet. His dusty brown boot pushed them one way and then back where they came from.

Again, he started to soften. "Hunter talked about that. He associated it with something I didn't understand. He got baptized. What's that have to do with anything? I don't get it. His wife, Piper helped him do that. She's a great person. And she just gave birth to Hunter's baby earlier this summer!" Marcus quit speaking, looked around and then continued in a shaky emotional voice while he kept his anger only partially concealed. "And no dad left in the world to help raise this baby girl."

The stranger continued in the role of impromptu counselor, a role she had not sought, but had instinctively accepted. This was not new for her. Sometimes out on trails during her years of service in the national parks, other times in coffee shops, or while she stood in checkout lines in grocery stores, she opened her heart's door and listened to people's pain. She had a history of enveloping troubled souls who needed to feel a hint of compassion from someone. From anyone.

Before she spoke, she used her facial expression to convey her concern. Then she exclaimed, "No dad around. That poor little baby girl! And what an impossible situation for this young mom. Did you say she is Piper?"

"Yeah."

"You told me Hunter was baptized. From what I understand most baptized people think we live after we die. I wonder if your friend Hunter thought that way."

In a cheerless and matter-of-fact voice Marcus replied, "He did. Yep, he did. He made that pretty clear. He talked about 'the gift of eternal life.' But I just don't see it. I wish I could, but I don't."

As he spoke three hikers, coming up from the direction of Chicken Spring Lake, accidentally interrupted the conversation. They addressed the lady. Overhearing, Marcus caught on that the four of them had talked over a campfire last evening. Marcus observed but did not speak. Instead, he sank deeper into an awareness of his damaged emotions gurgling inside, including his anger and his feeling of being miserably lost. Add to that a strange mixture of irritation that this odd woman had invaded his pain, but also gratitude for her presence.

The three interrupters departed down the trail. Before speaking, Marcus thought, *In the whole universe, I end up with this lady in this spot.* He slowly lifted his heavy, bowed head and said, "I don't know who you are, and I don't know how you did this. Here I am talking to you about my life, and I don't even know you. So, thanks, really, thanks, but I need to be alone now."

She said she understood and that she would pray for him. "I didn't get your name." He told her, and she responded, "I'm Lydia. It's amazing how we get out here in the backcountry and make connections with other hikers so quickly sometimes. It happens a lot. Maybe see you up-trail, Marcus. I certainly won't forget you."

She hoisted her well-worn pack and slipped her arms through its straps. "Bye," she said, "for now." He watched her traipse downhill through the narrow tunnel of granite boulders and green pines with their reddish-brown trunks. He thought, *Downhill sounds good. Life has been too much uphill lately. Rock Creek is down from here.*

What he didn't know was that Rock Creek was about to jerk him out of his introspection.

Twenty-Four

Marcus started to hike. All alone. As he tramped along, he avoided conversation with other hikers. He thought, *I can't believe I opened up to that woman like that.*

By mid-afternoon he had descended nearly 2,000 feet in seven miles and was closing in on Rock Creek where he planned to spend the night. He saw the creek, a steadily descending, narrow cascade at a ninety-degree angle to the trail. He saw where the trail and creek came together and thought, *that blue hat looks familiar. Oh great! It's her hat.*

Lydia sat beside the creek, studying the rushing water. Though this mountain stream was not wide, maybe 15 or 20 feet across, the runoff from the recent downpour resulted in substantially deeper water and a stronger current than normal for August. She glanced up, saw Marcus and spoke loudly over the quietly crashing natural racket of the river. "Hey, there's my new friend. Hello!" She stood up, calculated the creek a little more and said, "I think it's a rock hopper, even if a lot of 'em are wet. I've got pretty good balance. What's your opinion?"

Marcus said, "I have no idea. You're a lot more experienced with this than I am. You're the park ranger."

"*Retired* ranger. But I think we can do it." She expressed a confident "Yes!" with a fist pump and said, "We won't have to take our boots off and numb our feet in this freezing water! You wanna go first, Marcus?"

"No. You go. I'm the rookie here."

"Okay. Watch this," and Lydia stood and slipped her arms through her pack straps. She instructed, "Remember to unhook your belt and chest strap, just in case. There's an outside chance you could slip and fall. We don't want our packs pulling us under. Not deep enough today to worry about—well, maybe it is. It's just a good habit to get into."

Marcus said, "That's right, Madman told us that."

She repeated, "Madman! Has to be a trail name. A person has to wonder how he got that one."

Marcus replied, "Long story."

"Okay. Here we go." She stretched her left leg out for a first step. The damp rock wiggled a little. She steadied herself and planted her right foot on another rock, wetter than the first, but firm. She leaned on her trekking poles for balance. She exclaimed, "Pray for me!"

Marcus answered loud enough to be heard over the sound of the rushing water. "I'm not worried about you. It's my own rock-hopping abilities that might be a problem." He remembered that Madman said rivers can be more treacherous than bears and mountain lions.

She called back, "Then pray even harder, but don't worry. We'll be fine."

He watched, impressed, as this older hiker picked her way across with remarkable finesse. The water flowed and roiled beneath her experienced steps. Her crossing seemed to Marcus to be athletic, like a slow and careful choreographed dance across the emerging rocks.

She was past halfway when she came to a spot where she had to take one fairly long step to her next tiny island. With the water near the top of her boots, she hesitated, but like the old pro that she was, she studied her course. Again she planted her poles in the white, bubbling water and reached her left foot forward. A couple inches of water were flowing over the rock she chose, and it tipped, unexpectedly. Lydia's foot began to slide. She worked to steady herself, but her other foot also slipped.

Marcus gasped as the unthinkable transpired. Ranger Lydia lost her balance and toppled over. Unable to regain any stability, she fell in backwards, her backpack dragging her down into the rushing stream. As she went down, her left foot caught between two small, submerged boulders and twisted.

She cried out. "Ahhoooww!"

Marcus stared as she struggled in the water. He thought, *She's a ranger. She's tough. That must have hurt!*

He knew he needed to help her, but how? He froze, helpless. For a split second he was angry. *I don't want this stranger's problems eclipsing my purpose in being here. Wait! This lady's in trouble. What do I do?*

He knew he could not remain aloof, tangled up in his own issues. He had to act. He instinctively ripped off his pack and waded into the chilly water. He ignored the rock-to-rock pathway Lydia had charted minutes earlier. The freezing water engulfed his lower legs and filled his boots, all of which caused him to feel immediately cold all over and unsteady. He summoned up every bit of strength and agility he had. Fortunate for him and for Lydia, his lower body had gained a new toughness through his backpacking. He leaned into the rushing water as it rose above his knees.

Struggling toward Lydia, his foot landed in an unseen gorge between the submerged rocks at the bottom of Rock Creek. The water surged higher up his legs. He wobbled but persisted through the rushing flood. He ignored the biting cold. Although this journey was short in distance, it seemed interminably long as he battled his way closer to his flailing fellow hiker.

Lydia had already gotten one arm free from the pack. She desperately but expertly worked to finish the challenge of freeing herself from the waterlogged load that had the potential to drag her under the surface. Due in part to her years of experience and the more manageable depth of streams in summer, she knew she would escape the trap she was in.

But Marcus didn't know that.

He had heard stories about hikers who tragically drowned during attempts to cross swollen mountain streams. In the back of his mind, he envisioned this woman trapped under water, turning blue, and no one there to help but this inexperienced, grieving rookie with absolutely no river rescue experience at all.

When he reached her, he was amazed to find her still seriously unstable, but almost back up on her feet. Both felt an initial sense of relief as they clasped hands and steadied each other. Marcus searched for careful footholds while Lydia hobbled and quietly moaned along beside him.

She had succeeded in getting free from her pack, but the stream had quickly snatched it and started to carry it away. The protruding branches of a sunken log had snagged a shoulder strap. The pack bobbed up and down in the roiling current.

Marcus left Lydia shivering on the bank while he carefully maneuvered through the churning danger zone. He retrieved the soaked backpack and deposited it at Lydia's feet before he waded back through the gushing water to grab his own pack. He rejoined her on the far riverbank.

"Oh, I can't believe I did this. I've crossed so many streams. Why did this one get me?" she asked through chattering teeth. "I just can't admit I'm getting old."

Marcus thought, *Now what? This is not what I came out here for.*

Twenty-Five

"I gotta get a fire going," Lydia said, "I'm freezing!" She gazed at Marcus. "You're soaked too. All my fault. I'm sorry." She briefly buried her face in her hands, looked up and said, "Thank you for grabbing my pack! If I'd lost that, I'd have been in a terrible fix."

He replied, "It's okay. What else could I do? You would've done the same for me."

Marcus surveyed the scene along the river while Lydia inspected her soaked pack and its sopping contents. Four or five tents already stood among the pine trees. Streams of wispy white campfire smoke filtered up toward the sky, and the breeze carried the aroma in their direction. Men and women attended to camp chores like characters in an Old West movie.

Marcus said, "Look at them all wrapped up in comfy dry clothing. I'm jealous."

"So am I!" exclaimed Lydia.

Marcus said, "Let's grab one of these spots," and he took a few steps up the trail.

Lydia didn't move. She stood with her fists clenched at her sides. With teeth chattering, she stated, "You don't have to help this old lady. I can take care of myself."

Marcus stared at her with a baffled look.

She stared back for a long minute before she admitted, "Okay. I need help."

Marcus asked, "What do people do up here when their entire life is soaking wet? It's not like you can run to the backpacker convenience store and pick up a dry piece of everything."

His sixty-some-year-old companion shivered, chuckled and stated, "Well, I can't sit here in the nude and hold my clothes over a fire. It's wilderness, but it wouldn't seem right. Let's start a fire, and I'll cozy up close enough to start drying my wet clothes.

Marcus might have blushed, but not today. Instead, he gallantly offered, "I have a second pair of pants and a shirt in my pack. They're dry, unlike you. You can borrow them. The sun's goin' down, and it gets cold up here, fast."

Lydia replied, "Marcus, I hate to burden you. And you're almost as wet as I am."

"I'm half wet. You're all wet. I'll be okay. And you're injured."

She accepted the clothing. Marcus, still shaking with cold, walked off in search of kindling while Lydia changed as quick as she could. As Marcus walked through the trees, he thought, *I wish Meagan were here to take over this campfire like she did in Desolation Wilderness.*

It was dusk, but not dark. Marcus returned, built a teepee out of the kindling and struck a match. The bright little furnace crackled as it heated up. They moved in close and Lydia purred, "Mmm, that feels good!"

He said, "Might be mid-fifties now, but with this breeze and wet clothing, feels like December has blown in. Could get to lower forties tonight. Brrr!"

Another hiker showed up carrying an armful of sticks and logs. He said, "I heard you two went swimming." He dropped the wood beside their fire and handed Marcus a dry pair of pants. He said, "Use these tonight. Give 'em back in the morning." Marcus hesitated but accepted, said thank you and jogged into the forest to change.

He returned, and Lydia reported, "I got a good look at my leg. Not broken, definitely sprained, the ankle is. Not the first time. This is going to slow me down."

Marcus produced a dry elastic bandage from his pack. "We're going to use this wrap, and don't argue. It's dry." Marcus did most of the wrapping while Lydia told him how to do it right.

They used Marcus' tiny stove to heat up two freeze-dried chicken and rice meals, which smelled and tasted delicious and helped to warm their bodies and their souls. The evening campfire lacked the joyful comradery so often found even among strangers in the backcountry. The normal chatter they might have shared was extinguished by the pain in Lydia's ankle and the raw emotions caused by the turmoil in the river. Marcus willingly erected both tents while Lydia apologized again for causing so much trouble.

Her nylon tent was close to dry when they turned in. Another neighbor came up with an extra camping blanket and convinced them he wouldn't need it that night. Marcus gave Lydia his down bag, which she reluctantly accepted. Marcus wore all the dry clothes he had with him, including a warm stocking cap and gloves. He wrapped up in the borrowed blanket and lay down on his high-tech mat designed to catch his body heat.

The two woke in their adjacent dwellings just before sunrise. Both chose to stay cozied up a little longer. Lydia limped out first. The ankle may have improved slightly overnight but continued to send pain from her ankle to her brain with each step. Marcus soon heard her rummaging for firewood and forced himself to get up and out. They exchanged pitiful looks at each other, then silently restarted last night's fire.

"Marcus," she began. "You don't have to . . ."

He interrupted, "Yes, I do. You need help. I settled it during the night. Don't argue."

She looked at him in the way a wounded doe deer caught in a trap might gaze at a passerby willing to stop and set her free. As the fire began to provide warmth, Lydia asked a common backcountry question. "Marcus, do you have a trail name?"

"No. The guys I hike with, they call me names—not always nice ones—but no trail name."

Lydia responded, "Well, you're my trail angel. Can't call you that though; too generic."

Marcus said, "You must have one, out on the trails as much as you've been."

"I do." She chuckled and shook her head. "You won't believe this, but it's . . . Ms. Rescue. Yeah. Me! Can't miss the irony there."

"It's life, isn't it." He sighed and said, "I guess everybody needs to be rescued once in a while. I've needed it lately. I like to take care of myself without help from anybody. My girlfriend—Meagan is her name—she rescues me from my low times more often than I like to admit." He pulled a glove off his right hand and reached up to rub his forehead. "Here I go again, talking about me. What is it about you that makes me talk this way?"

Lydia was quiet, reflective before she spoke. She lifted her eyes from the campfire, stared off into the trees and said, "I've seen my low times. My life has actually produced a few pretty horrific chapters." She glanced at Marcus, then focused again on the fire and said, "Could I share a little philosophy I picked up somewhere?"

He said, "Sure. Go ahead."

Lydia said, "Personal pain can help people develop empathy for other people who are hurting. It doesn't always happen. It's easy for us to internalize the pain and become bitter, sometimes hateful. I don't mean to sound preachy, but"—she hesitated and then said—"God has helped me turn my pain into something positive, even productive. Maybe that will happen for you someday."

The fire glowed and added its unique aroma. A couple teenage-looking hikers walked by. Lydia spoke again. "Now Marcus, you need to go on. I've hobbled through life before. I can hobble my way up this trail and take care of myself."

He replied quickly, "No way. Sorry. You're stuck with me."

She let his words sink in and then said, "Aw, Angel Man. Or maybe, Heaven's Helper? I'm searching. You deserve a name that announces the unique person you are. You're strong, but you're peaceful. You bring peace to others. I'll find a name that fits."

Twenty-Six

They transferred a good portion of the contents of her pack to his and started slowly up the trail. When Lydia spoke, Marcus noted that her voice did not sound wimpy or whiney but determined and measured. "Marcus, I can't deny it, this hurts." She grimaced, grabbed a breath, and said, "Awful at times, but I can do it. With God's help, and yours, I'll limp into Crabtree Meadow and recuperate overnight. In the morning we'll be two tiny specks in the universe facing a giant. That crest to the east is big!"

Marcus thought, *And she imagines God helps us little specks. Whether God does or not, I will. I'll stay with her. It's hard to be alone when you're hurting. I'm not sure God stays with anybody.* They labored on, silent except for the tranquil crunching sound under their boots on the pine-strewn trail.

Suddenly, Lydia's face lit up like a mountain sunrise. "Hey, how about Blessed RPM? It would be unique!"

"Blessed RPM," Marcus repeated. "I have no idea what you're talking about."

"A trail name for you."

"Okay. But I don't get it."

Lydia said, "It's from the Bible. Jesus said it, and it fits you so well. It's you!"

He wondered, *Why has this happened to me, that I'm connected with this woman? For how long? If there's a God up there . . . I need help!"*

Lydia continued. "Jesus said, 'Blessed are the peacemakers, for they will be called sons of God.' Get it? Blessed R. "R" like the letter. Blessed R the peacemakers, the PMs. Put it together; you've got RPMs. Now add this. You've been a 'blessing' to me. I have more peace because you've helped me so much. So, this is it, Blessed RPM."

Marcus decided it wasn't worth fussing with her and conceded. "I suppose."

Just then, two colorfully dressed, nice looking female hikers around Marcus' age appeared on the trail to the north. As they approached, they dropped their chatter. Lydia excitedly announced, "This guy just got his trail name!"

They drew closer, and one asked, "What is it?"

Lydia almost shouted, "Blessed RPM!"

As they slipped by each other on the trail, the first girl raised a pole and proclaimed, "Hello, Blessed!" The other one finished it, "Hey, RPM," and they were gone.

Marcus closed his eyes, shook his head and thought, *Crazy.*

He and Lydia kept walking. Eventually he thought, *She's a distraction. Maybe I needed her as much as she needed me.*

The pain showed in Lydia's face as they started the grueling climb up to Whitney Portal junction the next morning. She told Marcus, "I can do this. With you and your ibuprofen, I will defeat this mountain." They battled their way hour after hour to the top of the crest and started down the other side. She said, "Down is easier, but not much." In her breath prayers, she thanked God for helping her struggle through the pain and for sending Marcus.

Marcus didn't pray, but he wondered, *Why did my trip up here turn out like this? I wanted to be alone.*

When they were within striking distance of Whitney Portal campground, they stopped, dropped their packs and sat down again to let Lydia rest. Marcus gazed back toward the jagged granite spires behind them. He listened to the breezes that were stirring the tree branches farther down the trail. He breathed deeply of the pristine backcountry air and thought, *There's healing in this. It's different than I expected, but I'm glad I'm here.*

Lydia's voice interrupted his thoughts. "Do you know about the hostel in Bishop?"

He said, "No, I don't."

She explained, "It's an overnight shelter used primarily by hikers on the Pacific Crest and John Muir trails. It's not free, maybe 25 bucks a night. Dormitory type rooms with bunks and shared bathroom facilities. We can hitch a ride from the portal to Bishop."

Marcus shook his head and said, "Oh, why not?" Before they stood up to start hiking again, he said, "Ms. Rescue, I have to tell you this. Maybe you rescued me up here. Thanks for hearing my story and soaking up some"—he breathed deep— "of my trouble."

She smiled graciously and said, "Trips into the backcountry often take unexpected turns. Surprises are kinda normal up here. But listen, you've taken a load of my trouble. You've been an angel to me, a trail angel, a blessing! You'll always be RPM to me."

They made the portal and appreciated the modern convenience of the outhouses. They started down the paved road and stuck out their thumbs. Their odd appearance apparently helped. Only two cars passed before Gus stopped. They threw their backpacks into the dusty bed of the old, blue pickup. Lydia limped into the front seat and Marcus took the back.

After introducing himself, Gus said, "Let me guess. That's your son back there, and she's your mom. Right? And you're limping. Did you get hurt on the trail?" Gus' scruffy, graying beard, old leathery brown hat and general appearance suggested he was acquainted with the backcountry.

"Nope, not my son. We met at Chicken Spring Lake," answered Lydia.

"I know the place well," said Gus. Then he chuckled and said, "This doesn't seem like your normal backcountry trail romance. I've had a few of those." Marcus looked out the window and rolled his eyes.

Lydia exclaimed, "Not only do we get a ride, we get a comic to go with it! And yes, I'm limping. I fell into Rock Creek. It was freezing! The stream was way high because of that big rain a few days ago."

"A gully washer!" exclaimed Gus.

"I'm still embarrassed that I fell in. But this compassionate young man stopped to help me. That was unfortunate for him because he got stuck with me. All I could do to pay him back was give him his first trail name ever. Would you like to hear it?"

Gus said, "Sure."

She said, "Blessed RPM," which resulted in a puzzled look on Gus' face.

She explained, "It's in the Bible. 'Blessed are the peacemakers, for they shall be called sons of God.' Marcus there in the backseat has been a huge blessing to me. He and I are both searching for peace. So, he's Blessed RPM. Blessed R, and PM for peacemakers."

Gus said, "I think I followed that. But hey, whatever. Happy trails back there, RP."

A weak "thanks" trickled up from the backseat.

Gus asked, "Where you headed?"

Lydia answered, "That hostel in Bishop."

"The Hostel California," Gus exclaimed. "I'll drop ya there. Ya ever heard how it got its name?"

She said, "Nope."

Twenty-Seven

On the way to Bishop Gus explained, "It was just the hostel until a group of PCT hikers started messin' with the words of an old song called 'Hotel California,' and it stuck."

Lydia listened graciously and moaned quietly.

Gus dropped his exhausted riders off after dark. Lydia's ankle felt like it was ready to fall off, and she wished it would. They knocked on the brightly colored door. A young man dressed in worn out hiking clothes opened it and invited them in.

Lydia apologized. "Sorry to be arriving so late."

"No problem." He said, "It's normal. But you've got a nasty limp goin' on there, young lady."

In a cordial but tired voice, Lydia said, "Not feelin' too young, but thanks for flattering an old lady." She released an exhausted sigh and asked, "How much do these bunks cost nowadays?"

He replied, "Sorry to say it, but we've had to keep up with the government's inflation problem. They're forty bucks a night now."

They paid, and the host led them into the clean but crowded dorm they would share with seven other PCT hikers and area rock climbers. Everybody's gear filled up half the room. Lydia took a bottom bunk, and Marcus claimed the one above her.

Marcus woke at sunrise and wandered out to the hallway. A lime green flyer tacked to a worn-out bulletin board caught his eye. "Free Breakfast. City Park. 1/2 mile from the hostel. 9:00 AM. Summer Saturdays." The flyer included a walking map. Marcus thought, *This is Saturday. I'm going. I'm hungry.*

He invited Lydia after she climbed out of her bunk an hour later. She opted to stay at the hostel. Gus said he would tote them up to Horseshoe Meadows to retrieve their vehicles and gave them his cell number with one condition. "Don't call me until mid-morning, like about noon."

Marcus, or RPM stepped out the front door. As he closed the yard gate, he glanced back and realized he had missed the full effect of the turquoise exterior paintjob, lavender gable and red front door when they arrived in the dark.

The morning weather was pleasant for August in Owens Valley. It could get hot this many thousands of feet below the trail. He found the park and occupied a bench beside the pond for less than ten minutes before a van pulled in. Breakfast started its transfer from van to picnic table. Marcus wandered over.

The gentleman who drove the van looked about Marcus' age and started speaking when Marcus got close enough to hear. "Hey man, come on over for some homemade breakfast. My guess is you're a PCT hiker, and you might be lodging at the hostel. If I'm right, then you would be experiencing hiker hunger this morning, and you would love to partake of the non-trail food that is trekking in your direction. Besides that, we love meeting PCT hikers. And hearing their stories!"

Marcus said, "You might *not* love *my* story, but other than that, you've got me pegged."

"Try me," was the quick response.

Marcus said, "It's a long story. I didn't plan to be here in Bishop or staying at The Hostel California. But here I am."

The young man said, "You're definitely not the first hiker who's shown up for breakfast who didn't plan to be here." The guy noticed that Marcus peered into the van and easily deduced the object that had caught Marcus' eye. "That's my old Martin acoustic. You a picker?"

"Yeah."

"Then pick it up and pick a little. You're probably about ready to go into pickin' withdrawals. How long you been hiking?"

Marcus said, "Just a few days."

The guy said, "But you miss playing. I can tell. Check out that Martin."

"Talked me into it." Marcus carefully cradled the well-worn guitar over to a lawn chair the guitar's owner had set up. He sat down and started playing modestly.

The guy kept after his unpacking, but then stopped to listen. When Marcus finished a tune, he said, "Hey, that's good! You could be, um, professional. Are you?"

"Parttime."

"Band?"

"Yeah."

"Name?"

"The Yearning."

The guy seemed excited. "Really? Really! I've heard you on social media. Good stuff! You all speak to the Trouble. Thank you!"

Marcus smiled, took heart in the affirmation, but thought, *Won't be the same without Hunter.*

More cars arrived. More food and plastic utensils found their way to the picnic tables. More people came, some on foot, a few on bikes. Some looked like hikers, others looked well kempt, like townies.

"Let's eat!" It was the owner of the Martin who said it.

Marcus couldn't help but stuff himself after several days of trail food. While he was still inhaling his third super tasty caramel roll, the owner of the Martin picked it up. A girl with a newer looking KoAloha ukulele joined him and brought another girl along with her. Then a guy with a forest green, wide-brim hat stepped up with a black Fender acoustic bass. They started picking and singing a blend of bluegrass and Indie-folk sounds.

Marcus was corralled. They played their instruments well and sang right on key. They sang their bluegrass songs off-key, as they are intended to be sung. He thought, *Hunter would have loved this. Jesus keeps showing up in the lyrics.*

They quit. Marcus didn't speak out, but he wanted to. *Keep going! That last one was so cool. Your music feels like sunshine breaking through the clouds.*

The guitar player addressed the small crowd. "You people should know that we have a guest here who is part of an up-and-coming prophetic band called The Yearning. Hey man, what was your name?"

Marcus answered shyly.

"Well, Marcus, thank you for what you do and for being with us this morning. Hey, people, we also have a pastor here." A middle-aged man smiled and lifted his hand. The Martin player went on, "James loves God, and he loves those Sierras over there. If you can stay a little longer, we'll find out what Pastor James has for us this morning."

One young woman rose from her lawn chair, apologized, expressed her gratitude for breakfast and strolled back toward the street. Everyone else was apparently glued, willingly so, to lawn chairs transformed into church pews in a pleasant Saturday morning outdoor sanctuary.

Twenty-Eight

Marcus thought, *He doesn't look much like a pastor, but what do I know about what pastors are supposed to look like? This guy looks more mountain man than preacher man.* James started speaking, and Marcus thought, *Doesn't sound much like one either, not like those guys you hear when flipping through channels. Doesn't look ancient either.*

Marcus listened as Pastor James began to read a list of sentences from his phone. Each one began with, "Blessed are." Marcus thought, *This sounds suspiciously familiar.* James read, "Blessed are the peacemakers for they shall be called sons of God." Marcus almost guffawed. *Great, it's Blessed RPM. Again! How could this guy come up with the same words as Lydia?"*

Marcus tuned back in and heard Pastor James speaking in clear and simple but profound terms about Jesus as a peacemaker. Marcus thought, *Pertinent topic! He won't have to work too hard to convince us about the lack of peace we're all dealing with.*

Marcus unintentionally tuned in and out of the pastor's words, but he heard James say, "With all the trouble today, we need peacemakers. The world has lots of war heroes; we can support and appreciate them. But we need 'peace heroes,' influencers who can turn down the heat that too often explodes into violence in our streets. Innocent people get killed. It's tragic."

Marcus thought, *Hunter! How could this guy know? Does he know Lydia? Did she tell him? She couldn't have. She's been with me constantly since I told her about Hunter.*

James' voice invaded Marcus' mental world again. "People know Jesus, but they miss the crucial fact that He was, and still is, a peacemaker. He's an in-your-face kinda peacemaker at times, but He's always been the Prince of Peace. His teaching is full of statements that would help people diffuse the hate, if they would only listen to Him.

"Jesus said the Holy Spirit would teach the truth. The truth is our nation needs an uprising. We don't need a surge of militant political radicals from either side. We need peacemakers who will lead us away from this senseless violence and killing. Where are those people? When will they hear a call from God and save us from the ugly predicament we're in?"

One of the breakfast guests who looked early twenties abruptly stood up out of his lawn chair and spoke loud enough for all to hear. "Pastor, you apparently have no idea how serious this battle is. Thanks for breakfast, but I can't listen to this. There's not gonna be any peace without massive change, and that change is not gonna happen without force!" He grabbed his backpack from where he had left it leaning against a tree and strode briskly toward the street.

James called out after him. "Thanks for coming, really! Be careful out there." He quietly spoke to everyone still seated. "Not the first time that's happened," and he resumed his talk.

Marcus could hear the pastor's voice, but his brain took off on a rollercoaster ride through the ups and downs of his unsettled life. He thought, *Peacemaking. I've dreamed about it since I was a child. I've tried to learn it.* Marcus gazed upward, above the trees. "Hunter, are you up there? Are you with me . . . somehow?"

The playground scene he experienced with Hunter in grade school, when gunfire erupted on the street, flashed briefly on his mental screen. He was temporarily back in the ICU with all those tubes stuck into Hunter's lifeless body. They were in Desolation Wilderness where Hunter heard Piper's whisper, and they were back at that house where Hunter was baptized in the backyard pool.

Marcus felt an emotion he couldn't understand, deep and mysterious, moving below the surface of his conscious mind. Pastor's words burst back into his ears. "You have heard that it was said, 'You shall love your neighbor and hate your enemy,' but I say to you, love your enemies."

Love your enemies? Marcus closed his eyes and slowly shook his head. *Where'd he get that? Nobody does that. It's impossible. We hate our enemies. It's natural. We even hate old friends when their politics make 'em look like enemies.*

Marcus struggled with his thoughts. He also felt a strange inspiration. James' voice caught his attention again. "We need twenty-somethings—and sixty-somethings—who will let Jesus mold them into powerful world-changers. They will not shoot guns at opposing political forces. They will take up what the Bible calls 'the sword of the Spirit.' They will help turn this country and this world back from the dismal, dark direction we are headed in today."

Marcus leaned back in his borrowed lawn chair. His arms relaxed and fell limp at his sides. He breathed deeply and let it out slowly. He soaked up the sunshine and thought, *Peace. I feel it, and I don't know why. I don't even understand what the preacher's saying. But Hunter would get it. We need peacemakers, not stray bullets.*

The talk ended, and Marcus thought, *That went by faster than the music, and it went by too fast.*

Twenty-Nine

Marcus nodded toward the pastor, mouthed, "Thank you," and turned to walk away. The young man with the guitar called out. "Wait, Marcus! I want you to know, I'm going to pray for you. In fact, if you're okay with it, I'd like to pray with you, like now, before you go."

Though uncomfortable with the idea, Marcus responded. "Okay, I guess so."

The young man said, "Before we pray, can I ask if you're a believer? I mean, do you believe in Jesus as your Savior?"

Marcus replied, "I'd like to, I think I would; but I'm not there. At least not yet. Not sure I ever will be."

The guy said, "Okay. Tell me more."

Marcus grimaced, gazed out toward the Sierras, then down at his feet. He looked up and said, "I lost a friend, my best friend from child-hood." He breathed deeply and exhaled slowly. "His name was Hunter. A stray bullet from a stupid political rally killed him."

Marcus heard the guy say, "Oh no, that's terrible!"

"Yeah," Marcus said and continued. "My friend believed. He got baptized. He talked about Jesus." Marcus turned his face directly toward the man. "He would've loved everything you people did this morning. But God didn't let him live long enough to hear it. He was only 22 years old." Marcus stopped for a moment, looked away and said, "I'm sorry to bother you with this. I . . . I don't know what's gotten into me. I keep telling everybody my troubles. And they're my troubles, not yours. Sorry."

The guy said, "Marcus, listen, God loves you, and I hope you'll understand this. God's not the villain." That statement echoed in Marcus' head as he wondered, *What does that mean?*

The guy went on, "God gives life. He promises eternal life. God is all for life." He stopped a moment, then asked, "What would your friend have loved about what we shared this morning?"

Marcus appeared to turn the question over in his head. Then he said, "You people talk and sing about Jesus. You say you love Jesus. Hunter was like you in that way. But hey, I need to get going. I need to catch my ride up to Horseshoe Meadows and retrieve my car. I'll see you later."

The guy looked sincere when he said, "Are you sure you can't stay a few more minutes? I think I could help you understand what it means to invite Jesus into your heart."

Marcus said, "Sorry. I've gotta go. Thanks again." He picked up his heartache and carried it to the street and back to The Hostel California.

Gus kept his promise and toted the two unlikely partners up to Horseshoe. They thanked him earnestly and offered him gas money, which he refused. His old blue pickup disappeared down the road as Lydia and Marcus stood and conversed on the gravel parking lot. One or two cars stirred up the dust as they drove past. Marcus caught the scent of marijuana as a couple walked casually by. The afternoon sun shone gently on the scene.

"I won't forget you, Marcus. You're a lifesaver, a trail angel, a blessing, an RPM!" Lydia smiled and winked.

He thought for a moment before he said, "I'll try to be an RPM, a peacemaker. That would be good." He pretended to get excited, pumped his fist, and half shouted, "Go, RPM, go!" He chuckled, but returned to his normal voice and added, "We know that won't be easy. And of course I will think about you, Ms. Lydia, Ms. Rescue. How could I ever forget this trip and the time you and I spent together?"

The two shared a heartfelt hug. Both grew teary-eyed. Both tried to hide their tears, and both did a poor job of it. Marcus told himself, *It's obvious that a strong connection has been made here.* They promised to stay in touch.

That afternoon and into the evening Marcus drove and used the alone time to process. He turned over Pastor James' words. He waded through memories back to college and Desolation Wilderness. He plowed on through the darkness and scattered artificial light toward his messy apartment on the west edge of Sacramento. He pulled into his driveway and said, "Man, I'm ready to be home and in my bed."

Not quite ready to doze off, he thought about the guy with the Martin and regretted he had not caught his name. The words about Jesus and peacemaking came back again and again. He wondered, *How could Jesus tell people to love their enemies?*

Thirty

The sun had been up a couple hours when a ding on his phone shocked him out of dreamland. It was a text from Rafa asking, "Where are you?"

"I'm back."

"Can we get together?"

"Come over."

He arrived, and Marcus sensed within the first minute that Rafa seemed pensive and edgy. He wasn't himself. Marcus naturally suspected it had something to do with the loss of their friend.

The issue surfaced soon enough. Rafa said, "I need to tell you this. I joined The Solid Society. I've attended a few training sessions, and I've picked up more protection. I know you're not in favor of people arming themselves for the battle, but the left is getting meaner and meaner. Somebody has to defend this country from them, and I plan to do my part."

Marcus thought, *More bullets flying around! Is that what we really need?* With frustration in his face, he said, "Rafa, you aren't gonna put this fire out with more gunfire. Why do you think you can create peace by expressing more hatred? It won't happen. Get your militant training and see what comes next. Innocent bystanders get caught in the crossfire, like Hunter. Is that what you want?"

"You're wrong, Marcus. They're the ones who keep stirring things up, and somebody's gotta stop them."

"Come on, Rafa. There has to be a better way." Rafa returned a calloused look.

Before long, Marcus could tell he wasn't getting anywhere and decided to alter his approach. "Listen, I have to tell you what I heard up in the mountains. I spent the night in Bishop at the Hostel California and ended up at a free breakfast at the city park. Good folks. Good music! Good atmosphere. This guy talked about Jesus . . . like Hunter used to talk about Him, like Piper still does. Isn't it amazing that Piper continues to say she loves God? You'd think she'd blame God for letting Hunter die. You loved Hunter, and you love Piper. You were there for her that day."

Marcus paused. Rafa slowly nodded tacit agreement, but his face remained dark and doubtful.

Marcus went on. "The guy read Jesus' words from his phone. Apparently, it was Jesus who said people need to 'turn the other cheek.' You ever heard that?" Rafa only gazed at him with a blank stare.

Marcus said, "It seems that Jesus told people back then to put down their swords and stop retaliating all the time. He said the craziest thing. He said, 'Love your enemies.' Imagine that. 'Love your enemies!'"

Rafa said, "I'm not going to love my enemies. You're my friend, and I'll listen to what you say. But I'm in a battle, Marcus, and I don't love people who would like to kill me. Darren used to pretend he was a friend. Not anymore. He's the enemy. He's joined the Local Liberties League, the Triple L. Just think of them as the Loopy Liberal Lefties. He's always been ultra-left, ever since we met him. Now he's getting ready for the war, and he's been building an arsenal for years."

An imaginary scene flashed briefly onto Marcus' mental screen: Rafa and Darren firing rounds across the lawn of the Capitol. At each other! Trying to kill each other! And barely a hundred feet from the sidewalk still stained with Hunter's blood.

"Marcus, I think you need to come to a Solid Society team meeting with me. You would agree with most of what this group stands for."

Marcus responded, "I'm not coming. Rafa, and here's a better idea. You come with me up to Bishop and listen to this guy talk about peace-making. That's what we need; it's what our country desperately needs."

Rafa grunted and said, "My new Glock pistol is my peacemaker. It's the only one I need." He let his statement hang in the air for Marcus' sake. Then he added, "It's too bad my uncle Carlos didn't have the protection he needed when they shot him."

A moment's hesitation, a concerned frown, and Marcus asked, "What happened to your uncle, Rafa?"

"I'll tell you. Tio, or Uncle Carlos Milagro was a strong conservative voice down in Venezuela. I never got to know him. I just heard the stories. He was speaking at a rally in the capital city of Caracas one spring. They say it was a beautiful day, lots of sunshine, cool breeze, flowers blooming. He was about thirty. My father was a couple years younger.

"The leftie liberals assassinated him. It's no wonder my papa doesn't have time for the liberals in this country when they killed his brother in Venezuela. They did it just because he had a strong voice and a growing following among conservatives."

Marcus said, "Oh, my friend, that's horrible. How did your family ever get through all that?" Though Rafa didn't answer, Marcus hoped he could feel the compassion he felt for him and for his family.

He continued. "But Rafa, do you think you might be painting with an awfully wide brushstroke when you connect what happened to your uncle in South America decades ago to what's happening in America today? It wasn't anybody here in the U.S. that murdered your uncle in Venezuela."

Rafa interrupted. "They're the same everywhere you find them. They push their 'progressive' ideas, which always hurt people and destroy the economies of entire countries, throwing the poor into deeper poverty. And when they don't get their way, they riot and kill people and burn neighborhoods down to the ground. They have to be stopped."

Marcus listened to his friend a while longer, then changed the subject. "Rafa, could we talk about Piper and the baby? You and I have reacted so differently to Hunter's passing, but we both care about his wife and baby. Did you hear how Piper picked the baby's name?"

Rafa quietly answered, "No."

Marcus told him. "Hunter suggested it before he left the apartment the morning he died. Piper named her Journey to honor Hunter's request and because the name fit a little girl going on a journey with a mom who never dreamed life would go as it did."

Rafa said, "I didn't know that. I sure want to help Piper anyway I can, but I don't know what to do."

Marcus said, "Same here. I'm so much less than what Piper needs me to be."

Their conversation soon died away. They shot each other questioning looks and said goodbye. Marcus thought, *I miss hooting like an owl with my friends.*

Thirty-One

Later that day he texted Darren. He was thinking, *I need to find out if my radical-left friend has fallen into the crazy zone as badly as the one on the right.* Darren quickly texted back. "Meet me tonight, 6:15 at Temple Coffee Roasters downtown."

Marcus parked his pickup near the corner of 9th and J streets. He reached for the silver handle of the coffee shop's glass door and was startled by an unexpected touch on his shoulder. He twisted his head around to find his old friend right behind him.

Darren said, "Change of plans. Come this way." The two shared a quick sideways bro hug, and Marcus fell in with his hiking companion on the sidewalk along J Street. Small talk followed.

"How's your mom? You and Meagan doing well? Of course you are. Getting married one of these days? You ought to." Darren seemed calm and cheery, but Marcus knew that reading him could be tricky.

Darren suddenly said, "Let's drop in here."

"The Sheraton Grand?" Marcus was puzzled.

Darren said, "Yeah. There's a coffee shop and a few other venues— well, the coffee shop is more like a bar. Nice comfortable place. Just follow me."

They entered through the elaborate glass entrance and crossed the stylish lobby. Darren led quickly down a hallway covered with patterned carpeting that never shows up anywhere but hotel hallways. Darren grabbed Marcus' arm, gave it a tug and said, "Come in here a minute."

He pushed open one of a pair of tall, dark wooden doors and walked through. Marcus followed uneasily and found himself at the back of a nicely decorated conference room. A quick survey revealed contemporary ceiling lighting brighter than needed and a stage at the front. Blue banners that embellished both sides of the platform boasted wording that he quickly guessed to be political mantras.

Marcus thought, *Darren has been on the opposite end of straightforward, and this is exactly where I don't want to be.* He picked up the commanding voice of the man at the podium. "We can alter the direction of this country . . ." The words trailed off into oblivion for Marcus.

"Darren, why did you trick me into coming in here?" he hissed. "You know I'm not gonna side with this group against my friends on the other side of all this political brouhaha." Though he was disgusted, he tried to speak as diplomatically and transparently as possible. "I love you, man, but if you wanted me here, you should've invited me instead of trapping me."

"Marcus, man, settle down." Darren gestured toward the crowd and said, "These are intelligent people. We could learn a lot about where our country is headed. Just listen." Marcus hesitated, irritated, but then reluctantly slid into one of the blue padded chairs beside Darren.

The speaker had obviously succeeded in commandeering the loyalty of the attendees in this crowd of three or four hundred. They applauded frequently. A gifted wordsmith, he presented his case. "Intelligent, progressive Americans in California and all over everywhere need to get busy. We must do whatever it takes to defeat these backward, conservative ignoramuses before they push the country back into the dark ages."

As he sat and listened, Marcus thought, *This guy reminds me of Professor Raging River. They both tiptoe around the idea of arming the left to go to war against the right. They understand how much militant language they can use without breaking the law. I'm going to listen only long enough to figure out how to pour a bucket of cold water on Darren's political bonfire.*

The speech went on, and the crowd followed obediently. "It is past time to try to legislate the kind of changes this country needs. The global transformation keeps growing and growing. Will America keep up and finally survive? The conservatives have succeeded in reversing our successes too many times. If legislation fails, smart people need to develop new methods. You, the Sacramento chapter of the Local Liberties League have played a leading role in recruiting and training world-changing leaders. But you know darn well that the battle has just begun!"

Marcus realized he had seen this rough-looking, red-mustached face on TV. This was Representative Ted Brogans from Oregon, a fire-brand known for his extremist activism. Marcus began to listen again as Brogans said, "Conservatives remind me of a bunch of cattle out in the pasture; they're so slow to get with the program. Somebody oughta drive them over to the packing plant and get rid of them."

Marcus left the meeting more concerned than ever about his friends. He thought, *Darren and Rafa are headed for disaster.*

Thirty-Two

Piper listened as Marcus poured out the latest news. Meagan sat beside him in Piper's modest apartment while Baby Journey, dressed in a flowered top and diaper, cooed and gently squirmed on her mommy's lap.

They had already spent a refreshing half hour catching up before Marcus brought up Rafa and Darren. "Please forgive me, Piper, for burdening you with this, but I'm frustrated. Is this the way we want our friends to react? They join militant groups that shoot real bullets at each other. Instead of working to stop the violence, they join up and get ready to do more damage. Losing Hunter is the worst thing that's ever happened to us. We miss him so much! How can these guys participate in the same fanaticism that stole Journey's daddy from us?"

Piper had to dig deep into her faith to stay steady in the face of Marcus' dismay. Before she spoke, she recalled a parable of Jesus. *A man dug deep and built his house on a rock. Vicious Storms came, but the house stood strong.*

She looked compassionately at Marcus and said, "Wow! I hate that about Rafa and Darren. We all had some cheerful times together, and it wasn't that long ago. Or maybe it was a different century. I don't know.

"But I know I can't control what other people do. I can control, with God's help, what I do when life gets rough. I can't control how our friends react to"—she stopped—"to Hunter's passing." Strong as she was, her emotions regularly stopped her in her tracks. She looked down into the peaceful, innocent face of Hunter's baby. She lifted her eyes to her husband's best man. She steadied herself until she was ready to speak a word of wisdom.

"But Marcus . . . we have to ask ourselves: how are we, you and me, how are we going to respond? With hate? Or with faith? You're not a hateful person. You're the opposite of that. Darren and Rafa are going to do what they're going to do. I hope and pray they change their minds. But Marcus, what are you going to do?"

Marcus was slow to speak while he carefully chose his words. "Piper, you just mentioned God's help. Hunter believed in God. Where was God that day? Why didn't God help all of us and keep Hunter safe? I'm sorry to bring up these questions, but I'm really struggling. I know you are, too, surely more than me." Meagan reached over and tenderly squeezed his hand. Marcus showed no visible acknowledgement of her gesture. He sat stone-faced with sadness.

Piper resolutely continued her attempt to dig deep. "I have asked those same questions. God knows I have. Why? Why Hunter? Why couldn't he have just come home that day? Why couldn't that bullet have landed a foot over and punched a hole in a building instead of stabbing this unbearable, painful wound into our hearts? Why, God? Why? Believe me, I have asked these questions over and over. When I can't sleep at night, I ask again and again."

Marcus inwardly questioned, *Well, what's God's answer to this one?*

Unable to hear Marcus' thoughts, but with an innate sense of what he was feeling, Piper continued. "I don't have all the answers, but I know this. God's not the villain. God has been with me hour after hour in the darkness of my shattered life, in the middle of my lonely nights.

God gave me this little girl, and I know that God did not cause that gun to fire that day at the Capitol."

She peered into Marcus' face, then Meagan's. "Listen to this from the Bible. Are you okay with me sharing a scripture?" Both nodded. Piper said, "A man named Job had ten kids, and they all died on the same day. Imagine that." Piper wistfully cuddled her adorable babe on her lap. "His wife told him to curse God for what happened, give up and die. Job refused to think that way. He told her, 'The Lord gives, and the Lord takes away.' Did the Lord kill their kids and take them away? Absolutely not. The Lord gives life and offers eternal life with Him. When this fallen, broken world is taken away from us, God gives a better world. Hunter is already there. I can't wait to see him again." Painful longing showed on her face. She asked, "Don't you?"

Marcus' words erupted like an uncontrollable groan. "I wanna see my friend." Meagan's wholehearted agreement was clearly expressed on her tearful, silent face. After several solemn moments Marcus made a transition. "Piper, you said something about the Bible. Can I tell you what happened? I heard this preacher in a park in Bishop. I went hiking up there." Piper thought, *did Marcus just said he heard a preacher? Did I get that right?*

He went on. "I met these great people and told them about you and Hunter and Journey. I told them that you would love what they were doing. They talked about Jesus the same way you and Hunter do. Oh . . . I'm sorry. I mean the way you do now, the way Hunter used to, after he started going to those meetings with you."

Journey squirmed, stretched a little and settled back into her mommy's loving arms. "So cute," Marcus said. He smiled at his friend's baby. "Anyway, this guy talked about the need for peace. He said Jesus was the biggest peacemaker ever. Do you think He was? If He was, what would He think about the craziness that took Hunter from us and is messing up our friends' lives? I'm sorry, I'm putting these big questions on you, and you're just trying to survive day by day."

Piper responded quickly, "No, it's okay. I'm glad you're asking questions about God. I've prayed for both of you so often."

Meagan blurted out with astonishment, "You've prayed for us? Shouldn't that have been us praying for you?"

Piper said, "Thank you, Meagan. You know I love you. You've helped me so much. I couldn't have made it this far without you." Meagan leaned over and took Piper's hand in hers.

Piper turned her attention back to Marcus. "Jesus is a peacemaker, probably in ways that we can't even understand."

Marcus said, "The preacher told us Jesus is calling people today to become peacemakers. What do you think about that?"

Piper answered, "Yes! Jesus can teach us that."

Marcus said, "I ran into this crazy woman up there"—he glanced over at Meagan and added— "like older than my mom." Meagan expressed her understanding by smiling and shrugging her shoulders. "Anyway, we hiked together a couple days. Long story. She fell in the river and twisted her ankle, really badly! So, I helped her."

Meagan said, "Sounds like you." She reached over with her free hand to hold his.

"She gave me a trail name. Blessed RPM."

Meagan's voice trailed off as she repeated the name to herself.

"She said it's from Jesus. Apparently, He said, 'Blessed are the peacemakers.' So, I was a blessing to her, and I hate to admit it, but she was a blessing to me, too. It goes like this. Blessed R, like the letter R. Then PM for peacemakers. Blessed RPM. Weird, I know."

Piper spoke. "Marcus, it's in your DNA, to be uh . . . an RPM. It's you. It's your make up. God knows this world needs more people who can calm things down." She let go of Meagan's hand and swung her arm back and forth. With an animated voice she declared, "The peacemakers need to rrrr-rev up their RPM's and get to work, like right now!" Everybody smiled and chuckled at Piper's attempt to interject a little Hunter-style humor. She became serious again and said, "We don't want other families and friends to go through what we're going through."

Piper shifted Baby Journey to her left arm and grasped Marcus' forearm. "Marcus, be a peacemaker. Grow into it. Learn it. Study it. Listen to what Jesus taught about it. Listen to what other people have said about it." She paused and then spoke with emotion. "Do it for Hunter!" Marcus looked semi-bewildered, but contemplative as he received Piper's words and watched a tear roll down her cheek. He wondered, *Did those words come from Piper or from somewhere else?*

Marcus and Meagan spent the rest of the evening at the apartment. Meagan snatched up Baby Journey for a little heartwarming cuddling. Marcus took a turn too. When she started to fuss, Mommy received her precious sweetheart back and nursed her. The baby made happy baby sounds.

They all reminisced. Much of it included Hunter. They remembered funny lines from their former resident comedian and laughed, not like they did back then, but they laughed.

Meagan suggested, "Maybe this baby will be a jokester like her dad."

They all stepped out on the front steps and Piper said, "Thank you for coming and bringing some love and healing for me and this little girl. Good night, my sweet Meagan, and goodnight, RPM, anointed peacemaker."

Thirty-Three

Bam! Rafa pulled the trigger. The bullet sailed, but not exactly straight. Rafa was no marksman from the Old West. His imperfect aim punctured the fleshy part of the left arm just below the shoulder of his intended prey.

A bloody wound in that spot would not have killed an enemy soldier, but it would have caused debilitating pain and taken the fighter out of commission for a while. Since it was a silhouette and not a real person, nobody cried out in pain. Rafa continued to practice and vowed to improve his skill for the sake of the cause of conservatism in America and around the world.

Daring Darren, as his new friends were calling him, was advanced beyond Deigo. He felt ready to prove himself as a valuable fighter in the worldwide battle, and the state legislature gave him an opportunity. Conservatives had gained enough votes in both houses to pass, just narrowly, a bill that would put greater restrictions on late-term abortion in the state. Such restrictions were common in other parts of the country, but not California.

Liberal leadership planned a protest outside the capitol building for Friday night. Conservatives planned to be there in support of the measure. City officials were concerned that the "peaceful" rallies could turn into an ugly clash. A police presence was prearranged, and the National Guard was alerted to standby readiness. Darren put it on his calendar.

Ted Brogans was scheduled to speak against the action of the legislature. Meagan heard about it and asked Marcus, "Was that the guy Darren tricked you into hearing?"

He responded, "Sure was."

Meagan said, "I remember you saying he likes to call people names, disrespectful names."

"What kind of state do we live in today?" Brogans was already half an hour into his speech on the steps of the state capitol. "Maybe some backwards hick place like Texas or Oklahoma or Arkansas or Mississippi might come right out and steal the rights of women, but California has stood firm against that kind of prehistoric numbskull insanity. We can't let this progressive state deteriorate back into the dark ages. We need to fight for the rights of women in this country."

Applause started with a ripple through the sizeable crowd but increased into a rumble. Brogans was drinking in the adoration he believed his rhetorical skills deserved. Darren whooped and then surveyed the area for any indication that a fight might break out.

A counter-protester lifted his voice and shouted, "Stop murdering the innocents!"

Brogans used his amplified voice to respond, "You can stop murdering the rights of women. Why don't you move your sorry carcass out of this beautiful state and take your ignorant ideas with you!" Brogans continued speaking loudly into the microphone, hardly pausing to take a breath. He had the mic, and he used it to talk over every other voice and dominate the present airwaves.

The day before the rally Meagan had forwarded a relevant post to Marcus. It read,

> Former Oregon representative Ted Brogans is a clear example of strong-minded speakers who have developed the technique of talking or shouting one another down. He has said he has no time to listen to conservative viewpoints because "they are wrong and need to be silenced and never heard from again." Brogans exemplifies the unfortunate reality that logical argument has come to be seen as an ineffective verbal tool in the growing hyper-polarization of America.

As Darren drove back to his apartment after the rally, he laid a hand on the holster still strapped to his side. He spoke out loud, "Hey, my carbon steel buddy, you never got a chance to leave your cozy little nest tonight, but the day will come. In the meantime, let's keep knocking down the silhouettes of those conservative clods at the firing range."

Marcus stayed holed up in his apartment that night. Near bedtime he thought about his two old friends. *Maybe I could call them together to talk things out. Nah! Maybe in the distant future, but at this point it would take a squadron of uniformed police to referee the event.*

Thirty-Four

What would Hunter think about his friends today? Marcus was walking. And thinking. The fall temps were still warm and the leaves still green. As he rambled through the muggy, tree-lined streets back toward his apartment, he called Meagan. "How can Rafa and Darren hate each other? We used to hoot like owls because we liked being together. Then Hunter was gone, and everything changed. Seems like Rafa and Darren are gone, too."

Neither spoke for a long minute while Marcus kept his walking pace. He broke the silence. "I keep thinking about Hunter's religious thing. Do you think that might help us? It sure affected him."

Meagan said, "Let's look into it. We could talk with somebody who knows more than we do."

Marcus said, "Shouldn't be hard to find, since we don't know nuthin'. Should we ask Piper about it?"

Meagan replied, "I don't think so. She has enough of her own troubles to deal with."

Marcus said, "Yeah, you're right. If Bishop were closer, I'd talk with the people I met in that park, if I could find them." He paused, "Piper asked me what I was going to do. It needs to be the opposite of what Rafa and Darren are doing, that's for sure. Maybe I could do what Hunter did and get more of God in my life. But how do you do that?"

They were both quiet before they started chuckling. Meagan said, "We have no idea, do we! But we could learn. We're not blockheads. We've been to college."

Marcus said, "Okay, we'll study it. Hunter was affected by those meetings they attended. We could go to meetings."

Meagan said, "There must be more to it than just meetings."

"Wait a minute, Meagan, somebody's beeping in. Hunh? Looks like it's Lydia, that lady I hiked with on the trail. I'll call you back." He made the switch. "Hello? Lydia?"

"Hi, Marcus. Sorry to bother you. I've been thinking about you. Hope I didn't interrupt you at a bad time. You doing okay? You've been carrying such a heavy burden on your shoulders."

"Well, since you asked, I'll tell you. My friends are ready to kill each other. So, not so good. And Meagan and I are just . . . well, our heads are spinning around. How 'bout you? And your ankle?"

"I'm good. But . . . you have friends ready to kill each other? I hate that. What's our world come to? All that makes my ankle sound minor. But I'm going for therapy and improving. I can drive, hopefully into Sacramento tomorrow. I'd love to meet Meagan. Would that be possible?"

Marcus answered, "She needs to meet you since she's heard all about you. How about lunch at the Yard House restaurant downtown? Noonish."

She replied, "I can do that."

Marcus said, "Great! There's no river you can fall into downtown. Just try not to get run over by a bus."

"I see you haven't lost your sense of humor, Mr. RPM. See you there."

He called Meagan back. "Can you do lunch tomorrow? Lydia, the lady I helped on the trail, wants to meet you."

She answered, "How could I miss that? Lunch with young Lady Lydia whom you pulled out of the river, I'm in!"

Lydia limped into the restaurant. Marcus thought, *She looks like a city-dweller, sort of.* She was all cleaned up, hair fixed, minor make-up, paisley shirt and new-looking black jeans. He thought, *I think she'd feel more at home perched on a log in the wilderness.*

He and Meagan had seated themselves at a table surrounded by well-padded chairs, a comfortable contrast to a rock in the backcountry. The table bumped up against one of the large windows. They could see out. No trees, just city.

They stood. Lydia and Marcus shared a brief hug. Lydia turned and stretched her arms out in the direction of Meagan. With an obvious but not overwhelming degree of discomfort, Meagan stepped forward and accepted the hug. They sat down, ordered sandwiches and began to talk about their recent life experiences.

They finished the food and sat sipping their coffees. Marcus wiped his mouth with his napkin and addressed Lydia. "From the day I met you, you've been easy to talk to. I was amazed. I told Meagan about it. You're a good listener, and I never told you how much I appreciated the way you shared your faith with me."

"Thank you, Marcus, and thanks for dragging me out of Rock Creek."

Marcus said, "We had quite a time, didn't we."

She said, "Yes, we did."

Then Marcus broached the subject. "Could we talk about faith?"

She smiled and said, "Sure."

"Lydia, maybe you're here today because Meagan and I have a problem. It's God. I hope I don't catch a lightning bolt for saying God is our problem."

Lydia said, "I think you're safe."

Marcus went on. "I told you about our close friend Hunter. Before he got shot, he got baptized. As a Christian. It turned out to be a good thing for him. I guess it didn't help him much when that bullet slammed into his chest. Well, maybe it did in some way I don't understand."

Lydia listened. She didn't interrupt, but when Marcus stopped talking, she suggested, "If your friend Hunter knew what Jesus taught about eternal life, we could say it helped him."

Marcus responded skeptically. "'Eternal life.' What's that? We hear the words, and we have no idea. People die. Like Hunter."

Lydia said, "I don't intend to clobber you with the Bible, but maybe I can help you understand some things. Please know that I have lots of respect for whatever religious philosophies you hold."

Meagan laughed quietly and said, "We don't have any religious philosophies. Of any kind. Sorry."

Lydia smiled and spoke gently but confidently. "Here's the most simple, well-loved verse in the Bible. Jesus said it. "God so loved the world . . . that He gave His only Son. Whoever believes in Him . . . whoever . . . will not die . . . will have eternal life."

The conversation continued. Questions. Gentle answers. Guidance, not pushy. Confident statements about faith. Affirmations about the positive changes that happened for Piper and Hunter. Beliefs about God. About Christ. About creation. More questions. Doubts expressed. How-can-this-be-? kind of questions. All three participated fully, passionately, respectfully.

Then Marcus said, "I'm going to step into the river here, and maybe the current will sweep me away this time, but I need to say this. I need more of God in my life. I want more of God in my life. I don't know how that happens. So, I'm asking. How do I get more of God in my life?"

Lydia pondered for a moment and prayed under her breath. Then she said, "Here's the first step. Say, 'Lord Jesus, come into my heart.'"

Marcus replied, "Okay."

Too quiet to be heard, Lydia whispered, "Thank You, Holy Spirit, for what You're doing here!"

Marcus said it. Out loud. "Lord Jesus, come into my heart." He smiled, humble and sincere.

Lydia said, "Say this, 'God, forgive me of all my sins.'"

Marcus said that out loud.

Lydia thought, *This isn't church, not a home group. It's a restaurant. Is this really happening?*

Lydia said, "Here's one more. Say, 'God, fill me with your Holy Spirit.'"

Marcus thought, *I don't understand what that means, but here goes.* "God, fill me with your Holy Spirit." He thought, *I don't know if I actually said a prayer just now or if I only repeated Lydia's words.*

Lydia said, "The Lord of all creation is responding positively to your open, honest heart, Marcus."

Meagan said, "I want Jesus in my life too. I hardly even know what that means, but Hunter and Piper said they asked Jesus into their hearts. If that means Hunter is up in Heaven, still alive somehow, I want that, too. If Piper is able to function as well as she does—I know she has her low times—but it's amazing that she's able to hold it all together as well as she does. If that kind of strength comes from Jesus—I know she says it does—I want it."

Lydia responded, "Meagan, God hears you. He knows your heart. He knows you want Him in your life. Just believe. Do you believe in Jesus, like Piper and Hunter do?"

"I can't say that I believe like those two. They are, or were in Hunter's case, so real about their religion. Their Christianity was, like, tangible in their lives. If I could have faith like that, I would want it. So, yeah, I believe. I choose to believe in Jesus." Meagan looked Lydia directly in the eye and smiled softly.

Lydia said, "You two ought to know there's a party going on in a place we can't see. We can't see it yet, but it's happening right now. It's party time! It's all because you two were just born into the kingdom of God."

Marcus cupped his right hand behind his ear and said, "I think I can hear the music." He gazed over at Meagan. "And I'm sure I hear a drumbeat. Don't you?"

She smiled and said, "That would be Hunter."

Thirty-Five

"We were born for this!" Ted Brogans was using his social media influence to whip up the emotional devotion of the true believers in the movement. Brogans had helped to form a coalition of groups that supported and promoted radical action against the other side. He never publicly endorsed the shootings, but several shooters claimed they had been inspired by his statements on his various media outlets.

In an op-ed piece one of Brogans' critics wrote the following.

He works carefully to keep himself out of the actual armed fray in the streets. Ted Brogans follows a long history of high-level government officials around the world who send unquestioning, patriotic young men and women into wars on deceptive pretenses. Like those top dogs, Brogans finds ways to keep himself and his own family and friends out of harm's way. He follows history's example of exposing other people's children to the unavoidable perils of appearing on those battlefields. He considers himself an indispensable general who needs to direct his street soldiers from a snug, sheltered position.

Both Darren and Rafa were paying attention to Brogans. Darren loved him and saw him as a key leader in the sociological battle. Rafa hated him and posted the following.

Friends, did you catch the latest from that progressive buffoon, Ted Brogans? He wants to put more criminals on our streets. He thinks convicts need less jail time and more "counselors." Our streets in California are already so dangerous your neighbors are afraid to step out their front doors. While he keeps himself safe inside his walled compound, he wants to liberalize the state's revolving door policies for our prisons, including Folsom. We would all be safer if the lawbreakers got their counseling inside the walls, not outside. Brogans is planning a rally to promote his crazy ideas at Central Park near the campus of U.C.-Davis next week, Friday night, 7:30 PM. I wonder who will be there to protest against this scumbag and his followers.

Friday night arrived. Rafa was there. Several hundred of Brogans' faithfuls were there, including Darren. About ninety of Brogan's opponents assembled across the street from the park where the rally was held.

The program started with a thirty-minute concert. The band was local, loved by some and not so much by others. They had put out a couple songs that pleased the progressives and alienated the more politically conservative music lovers in the area. One of their music videos included footage that had been shot at an earlier rally. A scuffle had broken out that night. The song lyrics hinted that the trouble was always the fault of those on the right. They finished their set with that song.

A young woman followed them and spoke about her incarcerated brother. "Yes, he committed a minor crime."

Online news sources reported her brother was caught along with four friends who stormed into a small, upscale clothing store in Sacramento. They held two workers at gunpoint and took several sack loads of expensive articles of clothing.

His sister told the gathering, "Look, my brother's a good man. He's been down on his luck, doesn't have a job. He had one but lost it and couldn't find another. He shouldn't be in jail. We need to thank God for great leaders like Ted Brogans. They are preventing California from becoming a police state."

A few others walked to the mic and spoke. Then it was Ted's turn. Someone in the crowd yelled, "Come on, Ted. Tell 'em!" Another echoed, "Tell 'em, Ted!" Pretty soon it was a chant, "Tell 'em, Ted! Tell 'em!" Ted waved his arms, indicating he appreciated the support but was ready to speak.

"It is good to be with you people tonight. You are on the frontlines of this battle. The future of this country is at stake. If we fail, the country fails. I know you are not going to let it fail. You will do your part, and trust me, I will do my part. I will be there fighting side by side with you for the future of America."

He went on, but within a few minutes a voice came bombarding from across the street. The conservative side protesters had erected an adequately powerful sound system of their own. With an accusing tone, it said, "Tell the truth, Ted. Stop the lies." Brogans was only briefly sidetracked. He was accustomed to heckling. He shouted louder. The other side did the same.

Then, *crash*! The liberal side threw a brick into one of the loudspeakers on the conservative side. An ugly crackling sound emitted from the speaker before it went silent. Members on both sides began to pick up rocks, bricks and bottles they had stashed around the area earlier in the evening. The shouting increased in volume and agitated intensity. Without any official starting signal, a participant threw a rock from one side or the other. Quickly, projectiles began to sail in both directions.

Rafa edged forward in the twilight, stepped off the curb, away from the row of small office buildings behind him. He took a few more short steps toward the crowd of nameless faces who had come to rally on the other side of the street. He squeezed the large rock he held in his hand. He kept his fingers off the sharp edge on one of its sides. Then with a grunt he hurled his rock-ammo across. He wasn't aiming at any individual, just the crowd.

But his missile flew far and hard and connected with a young woman. It nearly knocked her over backwards when it smashed into her face. Blood immediately gushed from her nose and forehead. A small scarlet shower flowed down her face and neck to stain her white and black checkered blouse. She fell to her knees, crying and moaning in pain. She covered her face with her hands. Two crouching figures emerged from the crowd, lifted her to her feet and half dragged, half carried her away from the front line.

Rafa was shocked. He had not thought through his actions. An unexpected anxiety rose up in his gut. He asked himself, *What did I just do? That was, uh, horrible. I didn't want to hit that girl in the face.* He took a few wobbly steps backwards. *I'm not sure about this. I shouldn't be here.*

He peered across the dimly lit street and saw Darren. He knew it was him. He was staring across the street from the exact point where the others had dragged the woman away.

Darren, unaware of Rafa, had seen the woman crouched down, reeling in pain. In his dark mind Darren conjured up the scene across from the Capitol where innocent Hunter's blood stained the sidewalk. His anger exploded inside him.

"Who threw the rock?" he screamed. "Come on out here, you coward!" No one stepped forward. Darren pulled his pistol from its holster, but kept it pointed toward the ground. He glared across the street at the detestable mob. He wanted to take aim and shoot. From the shadows on the other side a man dressed in camo drew his own pistol and pointed it at Darren. Rafa had already backed into the cover of the throng. The police fired their teargas cannons.

While he could still see, Darren's eyes darted away from the dispersing swarm on the conservative side of the street and toward the stage where Ted Brogans had been speaking. He thought, *What's Brogans doing now? We need him to show us the way here.*

But Brogans was nowhere to be seen.

Thirty-Six

Marcus heard about the trouble that broke out at Friday night's rally. He knew Darren would have been there, and probably Rafa. He had no knowledge of Rafa's rock throwing or Darren's drawn weapon. He decided to try a prayer. "God, I have no idea how I'm supposed to do this, but I have friends who need help. Thanks. That's it."

The thought of driving back up to Bishop wouldn't go away. Why that idea had gotten planted so solidly in his brain was a mystery, but he decided it had to happen. He thought, *Maybe that pastor has insights to help me rescue Darren and Rafa from each other.*

"Meagan." He had her on the phone. "I located the pastor I told you about. I'm going to ask him if I can come to Bishop to talk. I'm wondering if you . . ."

She interrupted. "Hey baby, you don't have to talk me into it. When do we load up and go?"

He said, "I'll call you back."

Half an hour later. "Pastor James invited us to come to the Saturday morning breakfast in the park and stay afterward and talk as long as we want. Let's jump in the truck Friday after work. If you can handle a roomful of smelly hikers and climbers, we can stay at the hostel." Marcus heard a tentative, "umm, well, I guess so." That was good enough for him.

He decided to share his plan with his mom. She had to repeat into her phone what she thought she heard her son say. "You're going to Bishop to talk with a pastor? Is that what you said?"

"Yes, Mom."

She said, "I guess that sounds like a good thing. I'm surprised."

Marcus answered, "Well, Meagan and I had lunch with my friend Lydia from the trail. We've both been feeling so lost since Hunter left us. But if Hunter were somehow able to see it, he would be one happy dead person. Okay, that sounds weird. But Meagan and I both decided that we believe what Hunter and Piper believe. It's Jesus."

Gloria responded like the many supportive but confounded mothers who struggle to understand their changing young adult children. "Well, if that's helping you, talking about Jesus and all that, I'm certainly not against it. Remember, I dropped you off at Vacation Bible School. So, I get a little credit, maybe."

"Mom, you get all kinds of credit. You've been my rock all along, and I love you. I look forward to seeing how this develops, and I promise, I'll tell you all about it. At this point I'm trying to figure out things like, well, prayer. That's a mystery."

Off the phone, Gloria said to herself, *Was that really my son talking about prayer? I suppose it could be helpful. It's been a while since I've thought much about God and church and all that.*

The weekend weather prediction was lovely. Meagan and Marcus were both inspired by the magnificent east side of the Sierras as they drove the truck south on 395. As they passed through one particularly scenic section, she said, "I'm wondering, did God make all this? Or is it the result of the big bang? Creation? Bang? Which? And if it's creation, are we supposed to learn something about God?"

Marcus gave her a puzzled look and gently shook his head. "Sweetheart, you're asking questions too deep for my little pea brain. But, yeah, I think mountains are God's creation. And I wonder if the glaciers carved out Yosemite Valley. That's what John Muir decided happened, which is different from God reaching down with His finger and carving out the valley. Whadda you think?"

She replied, "I don't know. I'm a rookie. But suppose it was a glacier that sliced through the surface of the earth and polished the walls of Yosemite Valley when it melted. Does that rule out the existence of God and God's part in creating the universe and the amazing things in it?"

He replied, "Umm, no."

She said, "Maybe it's a combination of both." She paused for a moment, then added, "I have an idea. Let's ask Pastor James about peacemaking, and then ask him how God made the universe!" Marcus chuckled and smiled.

They drove on, arrived at the hostel and quickly made a new friend.

Thirty-Seven

"Name's Nicolas, trail name Peace-Nik, rhymes with beatnik."

"Hi. I'm Marcus. Trail name's a long story, but I'm interested in your trail name."

"Nice to meet ya, Long Story." A wry smile, a subtle shake of his long locks and a wink from Nick. A knowing nod from Marcus, who thought, *Long Story would be an improvement over RPM.*

He and Meagan were all checked into The Hostel California. Nick told them he was part of a foursome of climbers headed for the Buttermilks in the morning. Meagan busied herself getting ready for the night. She laid her tattered old cloth sleeping bag out on a lower bunk. She decided the natural aroma from this athletic group was not overwhelming. Marcus leaned against the tarnished silver metal frame at the end of the bunkbed. Nick sat on his bunk a few feet away across the grey concrete aisle. He had thrown his top-of-the-line looking, well-used pack on the thin mattress. His ropes and gear were stuffed underneath the bedframe.

"What are the Buttermilks?" Marcus asked. "I'm not a climber, and I don't know much about this area."

Nick replied, "They're world famous, really. These huge boulders that we climb are so fun. A few of them are like five-story buildings, and the Sierra scenery is hopelessly beautiful up there, right at the foot of Mt. Tom. You might like it."

Marcus answered, "I would, someday, but, what about your trail name?"

"Yeah, that. Here's the deal." Before going on, Nick extended a quick stretch of the rock-hard, rock-climbing muscles in his arms, took a deep breath and breathed out the beginning of his answer. "Ahhh decided to write a thesis on Mahatma Gandhi when I was in college. I minored in International Relations and found myself caught up in Gandhi and his philosophy. He succeeded in freeing India from the empire, the British Empire, without a war, which is amazing."

Nick leaned forward and stretched his lean form up to a standing position at the end of his bunk. "No violence. Think of it." He brought his hands together, level in front of his chest, then threw both arms out to his sides, like an umpire calling a runner safe on base. His left elbow just missed the gray frame of the upper bunk. Instead of yelling, "Safe," he quietly exclaimed, "Freedom from the empire, without a full-scale war!"

He calmed down a little, but remained standing and admitted, "Well, not all the people in India followed Mr. Gandhi, but they were a minority. The majority followed the principles of non-violent resistance and got free from the British in 1947. Gandhi led the rebellion and constantly called people to reject violence as a means to an end. It worked. India is free.

"Dr. Martin Luther King, Jr. patterned his social revolt in the South after Gandhi's teachings. It worked there, too." Then quietly, but with passion, in a loud whisper he restated, "It worked!" His face took on a more thoughtful appearance, and he looked Marcus directly in the eye and declared, "It would work today. Yes, it would."

A veneer of consternation took over Nick's face. He shook his head as if in disbelief and added, "That is if these big-brained influencers around the world and here in California would quit inciting their followers to shoot their guns and throw their little bombs at each other." His face took on an apologetic look before he said, "Now you've been bombarded with more of the story than most people who ask about the Peace-Nik. But it's your fault. You got me started."

Marcus replied, "I'm interested. I really am. And for good reasons."

"Okay then, listen to this one quote. After that, we can talk about the Sierras. Gandhi said, 'Nonviolence is *not* a weapon of the weak. It is a weapon of the strongest and the bravest.' Dr. King and our oppressed brothers and sisters in the 1960s applied this principle. They demonstrated courage and strength when they chose peaceful protest over brutality. They made that choice while the cops beat them with nightsticks and threw them in paddy-wagons and hauled them off to jail. That took incredible self-control!

"Where is our Dr. King today? We need him, or lots more like him in our streets and fewer of these Ted Brogans types. Brogans is on the liberal side, but both sides have them."

"So true," was Marcus' informed response. "But Nick, I have to ask, do you ever go to the Saturday morning breakfasts here in the park?"

He responded, "I do that occasionally. My climbing crew won't go. They'll wanta be up at dark-thirty to climb. But I'll give it a thought. I might go tomorrow. I think a lot of Pastor James. You going?"

Marcus said, "Yeah, that's why we're here."

"That's why you're here?" exclaimed Nick, "For a church breakfast in the park? So, you are a couple Jesus radicals, aren't you. Or maybe it's just that you like . . . to eat?"

Marcus chuckled and said, "No! Well, yeah, we like to eat. But we're not radical, not about eating or about, you know, Jesus. We aren't now. Maybe in the future. This is all new for Meagan and me."

Nick turned his head toward her. "Meagan! We've yet to be introduced. I'm Nick the Peace-Nik, rhymes with beatnik."

"Hi, Peace-Nik. I'm Meagan. Rhymes with vegan, sort of."

"Ha ha! Jesus Radical, I mean Long Story, you've got a girlfriend with a sense of humor." Then back to Meagan, "Are you vegan, really, Meagan?"

She smiled, shook her head and said, "Well, maybe, actually, no."

"She's needed a sense of humor and a lot of patience to put up with me," Marcus said. "She's great, and she's helped me so much. Now we're here on a quest. We hope to learn how to be"—he searched for the word—"well, Christians, not fanatics, just people who know more about God and religion than we know now. We'd also like to learn how to bring a little more peace to our troubled planet."

"Oooo, my kind of crazies!" was Nick's enthusiastic response. "Jesus-peacemaker-people, all wrapped up in one. What a find! I hope we can be friends. And we need to listen to my friend, Pastor James. He's the right guy to talk to. He's smart, dedicated and committed to the culture of Christ-centered peacemaking, so needed today.

"But, one thing, let's not get sidetracked with 'religion.' That word carries too much unwanted baggage. What we want is Jesus, His teachings and a relationship with Him. But please, tell me how you got to be peace-loving, Jesus people."

So, with help from Meagan, Marcus told Nick about his childhood friend Hunter, about backpacking with Rafa and Darren, about Hunter's death and about the radicalization of the other two.

Nick's story was different, but there were parallels and overlap. All three told of their experiences. They eventually moved outside in consideration of the climbers and PCT hikers who had settled into their bunks. Nick led them to a small cluster of weather-beaten chairs next to a rickety old wooden fence on the edge of the property.

Meagan asked Nick about the fence. "The slats are alternating colors: pink, maroon, green, orange. How'd that happen?"

Nick asked Meagan, "Know what a zero-day is?"

"Nope."

He explained, "Long-distance hikers can rack up like thirty-five miles a day. When they get totally worn out, they take a zero-day. Zero miles. A couple years ago some artistic hikers took a rest here, got bored and needed a project."

Meagan replied, "Now we know," and smiled. After another hour of storytelling, she said, "I feel so at home out here this evening. It's cool and quiet, and I love the moonlit shadows of these trees. Me thinks we're gonna have a short night, but I'm okay with that."

Nick asked, "No regrets?"

Marcus answered, "Not a one."

They left their cozy bags and bunks early enough to get to the park. The guy who owned the Martin guitar sat down with them as they all partook of the tasty homemade egg casserole and colorful fruit salad. He said, "I remember you. About a month ago. The Yearning. That's your band, right? Great to see you again."

Marcus replied, "Great to be here again."

After a few minutes of small talk about weather, the mountains and music, the guy asked, "Would you play one tune with us? It's a praise song, an original. Easy, especially for you. The chords are one-four-five, key of G. There's an E-minor-7, of course. I can show you before we play."

Marcus frowned and answered, "But what about my eggs?" The Martin guy smiled. After the eggs and caramel rolls, the ukulele player told Marcus that Randy, the guy with the Martin, wrote the song. She explained, "It was inspired by a verse in Ephesians."

The song went like this.

> To the praise of the glory of God's grace
> Let our lives be
> To the praise of the glory of God's grace
> Sons and daughters
>
> Adopted children
> Brought to Him
> Rescued from sin
> By the blood of Christ.
>
> Grace poured on us
> God loved us
> And chose us
> Before there was a world
>
> Look what You have done
> Through the suffering of your Son
> You've blessed us with every spiritual blessing
> So all can see your love

Marcus played a Stratocaster that Randy brought to the park. His work on the Strat added to the texture of the song and even to its spiritual depth. This was a first for Marcus, using his gift as a way to worship the Lord. He felt a power in it, not only in the music, but something much more far-reaching. He wanted more of it.

Thirty-Eight

Pastor James sat down, thanked the musicians and cooks and the guests for coming. They made an eclectic assemblage of hikers and townspeople, some older, some younger, various ethnicities, a pastor and two new believers.

James introduced his devotional with a story. "Two little boys got into a scuffle. They were brothers. Both were in the wrong, but the younger got the worst of it. Mom scolded them both for fighting and told them they needed to forgive each other.

"The older boy reluctantly said he was sorry. The younger one only pouted. At bedtime Mom asked him if he had forgiven his brother. He responded adamantly. 'No!'

"She told him, 'The Bible says, "Do not let the sun go down on your anger."' The little guy listened with a sour but thoughtful face. The wheels were turning in his head. He finally looked up and innocently asked, 'But Mom, how can I keep the sun from going down?'

"He wasn't about to give up his anger. Too often we act like him. We get ourselves into a rage, and the last thing we're going to do is let it go.

"Here's a couple verses from Proverbs 15.

A few vegetables where there is love are better than the finest meat where there is hatred. A person with a bad temper stirs up conflict. But a person who is patient calms things down.

"Do we want to be hotheaded instigators and stir up trouble? Or would we do more good as capable diplomats who calm things down? Here's more from that same chapter.

A gentle answer turns anger away. But mean words stir up anger. . ... A tongue that calms is like a tree of life.

"And 'calm' isn't weak. Neither is gentleness. Jesus was unruffled enough to sleep through a storm in a boat! In His own words, He was 'gentle and humble in heart.' Yet He possessed enough otherworldly authority to command a storm to be quiet. He was so bold He could stand toe to toe with those who had the power to get Him crucified. When they succeeded, He endured the scourging and carried His own cross halfway to Calvary.

"Besides that, a weak person doesn't influence the whole world, which Jesus did. Listen to this from H. G. Wells, who said,

I am an historian, I am not a believer, but I must confess as a historian that this penniless preacher from Nazareth is irrevo-cably the very center of history. Jesus Christ is easily the most dominant figure in all history.

Nick raised his hand and began waving it back and forth energeti-cally. James recognized him and sounded like a patient teacher with his drawn-out "Yeees."

"Would it be okay if I threw in a great quote from a wise teacher, Gandhi?"

James answered, "Okay."

Nick said, "Pastor James, you reminded us that Jesus called Himself gentle. Brother Mahatma—not a Christian brother, I know, but a wise teacher said, 'In a gentle way, you can shake the world.' Gandhi shook it, and Jesus did a million times more. So, it's possible to shake up the world without getting mean."

Pastor James smiled, gave Nick a thumbs up and went on. "Jesus did not use up His days on Earth building a mean military machine. People wanted Him to do that and overthrow the Romans. He could have, but He didn't. A man whose words drew thousands upon thousands to hear Him could have stirred those oppressed people to start a revolt. Imagine a field general who could command the weather, raise his soldiers from the dead and heal every wound. Sign me up!

"He chose a different direction. He built a spiritual army that kept multiplying after he was gone and changed the world, without using violence. People who called themselves Christian eventually devolved into violent behavior and did it in His name. But that was never the true Spirit of Jesus.

"But don't ever think Jesus sat back and let evil take over. He constantly confronted the darkness that had taken root in people's hearts and minds. Today Christian peacemakers continue the same spiritual battle.

"They understand controlled use of force is sometimes needed to retrain evil. But powerful leaders too often and too quickly choose harsh force. Imagine a world in which those in authority understood and applied the teaching of Him who is the highest authority. The world would be better off if you and I did the same."

Thirty-Nine

James finished and immediately got busy helping clean up around the park's picnic tables. After dropping the last used paper plates and napkins in the trash barrel, he invited Marcus, Meagan and Nick to come sit with him. A large oak provided a shady spot with spreading green branches that hung over a circle of turquoise and yellow canvas lawn chairs.

Marcus and Meagan held hands as they walked across the green grass. Meagan kept enjoying the natural beauty of the park and only glanced at Marcus as she said, "I loved what Pastor James said. It's a message everybody oughta hear."

Marcus agreed. "More Jesus-style peacemaking would mean less senseless killing in our streets."

When they caught up with James, Marcus said, "Thank you for the sermon. Like I told you on the phone the other day, we wanted to come up here because we're curious about peacemaking, and also about the Holy Spirit."

Meagan added, "Ditto to what my boyfriend said. And if you can explain how God made the world, we'd like that, too." She smiled at James.

He repeated, "'How God made the world.' You think I'm smarter than I think I am."

Meagan said, "We probably have too many questions."

James responded, "We should have questions about God."

A couple birds cackled and flew from one tree to the next above their heads. The four sat down, and James started. "Let's talk about the Holy Spirit first. Marcus and . . . is it Meagan?" She graciously nodded in the affirmative. He smiled and said, "And Nick is here. He's already quite knowledgeable about the Spirit." Nick gave a thumbs up and grinned with the enthusiasm that seemed to be a constant stream in his life.

James said, "Jesus taught that the Holy Spirit helps us make the most of life. And He said we can be baptized in the Holy Spirit. But I'm wondering if you two have been baptized in water."

"No," they both said at once. After a moment Meagan spoke up. "Our friend Hunter who died got baptized. We were there. It was very cool and beautiful in a way, but basically a mystery to the rest of us."

James spoke gently. "Our worship leader, Randy told me about your friend. I'm sorry he was killed. That must be heartbreaking for both of you."

Meagan continued while the others listened intently. "Hunter was always a great guy, always fun to be with." She paused, and that familiar sadness flickered across her face. "But a couple years before he died, he started going to meetings with Piper who became his wife and the mother of his baby. She's a great Christian person. It's amazing to see how she stays strong with all she's gone through."

James picked up on what Meagan said about Piper. "The Holy Spirit does that today. He gives people strength to handle what they can't handle on their own. I have a question for all of you. What's happening in your lives that you think might require more strength than you have right now?"

Marcus slowly shifted himself in his lawn chair and leaned slightly forward. No one else had spoken, so he did. "Pastor James, I had a dream when I was young. I was only nine. There was a shooting in the street in front of our elementary school. That wasn't a dream; that was real. It happened during recess. Fortunately, they missed. No one was injured, not physically anyway. Emotionally, yes.

"That night I finally fell asleep and had the dream. A violent wind suddenly stirred up the lake at the edge of town. Hunter was out there, in a tiny boat. He's our friend that was killed. In my dream he was in serious trouble and sure to drown.

"But I spoke to that storm. I told it to calm down. And it did! It was like I had this unexplainable power over the wind and those huge waves. Hunter was safe. I remembered the dream when I woke up and still remember it today." He paused, looking amazed and perplexed at the same time. "I knew it was only a dream, but I wanted so much to be able to tell the storms of trouble that surround us to stop."

Meagan jumped in. "So true. We've got this tornado of trouble, and it's tearing us all up. Our friend Hunter was just one of so many who have been injured or killed. It's terrible in Sacramento. It needs to stop."

Nick had something to say. "The Holy Spirit can help! People all over the world want peace. They don't want all this trouble. They want to go to school, earn a living, raise a family. Most people hate this trouble. It's a minority that keeps the violence going in the streets. They think they're making the world a better place. They're not.

"Our pastor gave us a couple verses about people who stir things up. They oughta stir things down, if you can say it that way. And Marcus, you're a guy who could stir up the calm. You could do it! You could stir down the trouble."

Pastor James said, "Thanks, Nick. Good stuff! We all need the help of the Holy Spirit, and He wants to help us."

Marcus thought, *The Holy Spirit? Tell me more.*

Forty

Marcus and Meagan discovered that the Holy Spirit comes through un-expected channels. He apparently decided to show up in the form of a band.

Randy the guitar player was waiting by the picnic tables when the others finished up with James. He caught Marcus and asked, "Did you say you live in Sacramento but work in San Francisco?"

Marcus said, "Yeah. You have a good memory."

Randy said, "There's a band in the Bay Area, a dynamite Christian band. We're friends. I told them about you. They know your song, 'Hear Me Hear You.' They'd like to meet you. They're not as well-known as The Yearning. They're new. But they have what I would call a prophet-ic spiritual voice. They address the Trouble, like the Yearning does, but their approach is different. They're Christians, Spirit-filled and anoint-ed. Their lyrics are often bold, like prophets from the Old Testament. They aren't afraid to challenge the status quo. They challenge people and politicians alike to repent, to change. This band has that kind of courage."

Marcus had to be in San Francisco on Wednesday. He asked Randy to set something up. Randy got on it and also forwarded a sample re-cording from the band. Marcus liked the music and the lyrics.

The Lord says I will do something new

Now it will spring up right next to you

Will you even see it? Will you be aware?

When I make a way for you, will you be there?

The Lord says I will do something new

Come walk with Me and see what I will do

I'll transform kingdoms, I'll challenge the norm

I'll build up bridges, I'll calm the violent storms

Storms that are coming, terrors yet untold

Long for your salvation. Be rescued from this cold

Will you come with me? Right by My side?

Or just sit there, confused by all the lies?

After they listened, Meagan said, "I'm not planning to sit there and get confused by the lies."

Marcus said, "Nor am I. James told us the Holy Spirit will help us. Remember that scary night in Yosemite when I stood between that stranger and Darren? They both pulled their guns."

Meagan shuddered. "I remember."

She thought Marcus first looked worried but then calm as he said, "Where did the words come from? I know that was beyond me."

Meagan asked, "Remember what Randy told us about the band in the Bay Area? They're Spirit-filled and anointed, whatever that means. We get to meet these characters on Wednesday."

Marcus said, "Yeah, but Wednesday seems like it's a month away."

They drove together down to San Francisco and found the practice studio. A tall young man with long, light brown hair greeted them and introduced himself. "I'm Elijah Cummings. Good to meet you, Marcus."

"Hi." Marcus offered his trademark half-shy smile. Then he quickly and warmly turned toward Meagan and said, "This is my girlfriend, Meagan." He put his arm around her back.

Elijah said, "Hi. We've been super impressed with this guy's music. The Yearning has been a band on the horizon, headed to a higher level."

Marcus quietly said, "Thanks." Meagan could sense her boyfriend's conflicted feelings about his band.

Elijah continued, "Our mutual friend up in Bishop—isn't that a beautiful place—but what he told me wasn't beautiful. He told me your drummer was killed by a stray bullet at a political skirmish. I can't imagine how hard that has been for all of you."

A short, awkward silence followed before Elijah continued. "We have a vision, hopefully from God, to do our part to speak truth to the brokenness. So, we named our band after a minor prophet in the Old Testament. We are Habakkuk Band. I have to tell you—and this is funny, it is to us anyway. Sometimes people hear our name and say, 'Habakkuk Band. That sounds like a back-up band.'" The other musicians grinned knowingly.

Marcus smiled as he glanced around the circle and said, "Hey, I'm in the majority for a change. I thought the same thing: uh back-up band. How about you, Meagan? Ever heard of Habakkuk?"

"Nope. Sounds like a back-up to me."

Marcus' mind temporarily drifted off into his infatuation with Meagan. He loved the way her blue eyes sparkled with amusement at the conversation. He thought, *I'm so glad she's here. She has helped me so much. What a gift! What a beautiful gift, both inside and out!*

Elijah went on. "We decided we are fine with being the back-up band. In fact, we've heard it enough that we decided to adopt it as our unofficial motto. We are Habakkuk Band, the back-up band that backs up the truth in a world of lies."

"Ooo, I like that!" Marcus exclaimed.

Meagan expressed herself with two thumbs up. Then directing her attention toward Elijah and the band, she said, "People need a voice that speaks the truth. We hear too much half-truth, misleading talk that pulls people into a dark hole. A.I. technology has made it trickier than ever to figure out what is true and false.

"Two of our closest friends have gotten fooled and sucked into one of those holes. Hard to believe, but they've become polarized street soldiers. On opposite sides. We're afraid they are so far from reality they could kill each other. And one of them, Rafa was in The Yearning! He played bass and added so much energy and creativity to the band."

Marcus sounded discouraged when he added, "Yeah, with Hunter gone and Rafa playing street soldier, looks like The Yearning has lost that horizon you spoke of a minute ago."

They could tell Elijah wanted to respond but waited. His genuine compassion was impossible to miss. He finally said, "Marcus, I don't know that you'd be interested, but the four of us have agreed we would love to have you sit in with us." The other three musicians expressed agreement.

"We wouldn't expect you to make a long-term commitment, but it's something we could try. We'd want you to know up front that music is more than music for us. We work hard to get the sound right, but we deeply desire, and we pray we can become a prophetic Christian voice in this area.

"When we practice, we don't just practice. We take time in prayer, even fasting, and we share with each other what the Holy Spirit is teaching us. We read the Bible together. We do our best to submit ourselves to what we believe the Holy Spirit is showing us. We have a long way to go, but we're committed to this path."

Marcus didn't know what to say. He thought, *Music, the Holy Spirit and the Bible all wrapped up in a bundle. Wow! This would be a step down in notoriety from The Yearning. There'd be less financial reward.* As he contemplated the losses, he suddenly saw himself back in Bishop playing that one praise song in the park, and he felt that deep spiritual feeling again.

He asked, "Can I think about it?"

Elijah replied, "Of course. We would expect that. We hope you'll . . . pray about it too and ask for God's guidance."

Marcus said, "I will."

He appreciated Elijah's vision and confidence, and his face lit up when Elijah suggested, "How about sitting in on a couple songs before you go?"

"Yeah, why not?" Marcus looked over at Meagan, "You okay with that?"

"Sure. I want to hear these guys!" She grinned at Marcus and added, "Well, I wanna hear you, too, but, well, you know . . ." Marcus faked an offended face and teased, "You don't care if you hear me. I might cry like a baby." Everyone laughed.

Meagan said, "Crank it up, guys! You too, Marcus."

When they left 45 minutes later, he was flying high. They talked excitedly about the possibilities on the way back to Sacramento. He dropped Meagan off at her place and went home, but not right to sleep.

Okay, I'll pray, he thought. *Don't know much about that, but I'll try.* "God, You up there somewhere? I'm just learning about this. Please be patient with me. Is this right? Should I join this band?"

When he opened his eyes in the morning, he knew the answer. In text to Elijah: "I prayed, and if I heard anything, it was, 'Dummy, don't let this slip by.' The answer is YES!"

So, the path of Marcus Paver was paved toward true Christian discipleship with a band of brothers deeply committed to Christ.

Forty-One

The next year passed with its ups and downs; the new band was an upper. On the downside they missed their friends, not only Hunter, but Rafa and Darren. Marcus reached out occasionally. Rafa would say he was busy. Darren said nothing.

Habakkuk Band turned out to be more than they imagined. The music blossomed as they responded to an abundance of invitations to play in churches and outdoor rallies in parks and a few mall parking lots. Marcus was surprised by how many people his age and younger attended those events and filled those churches. He was amazed at how the band and the people became energized by this music.

He also became a sponge that constantly soaked up the Christian teaching he heard from Elijah and the band and at church. His life was changing for the better. His Habakkuk friends helped him see how the Holy Spirit works in our lives before we even know it.

Meagan was thinking, *I'm sure happy for Marcus and these spiritual break-throughs. But will there ever be a breakthrough in our relationship? That verse in Romans says, "tribulation works patience." I think Marcus is my tribulation! Great guy, but as slow as a bicycle going up a steep hill. I don't know how much longer I can wait for him to come around.*

He came over for supper one evening, which was common. He brought candles, which was uncommon. He set them on the table in her little dining room then moved them to the bookshelves, TV, coffee table, wherever he found a level, fireproof spot. He brought a guitar, which was not unusual.

The sweet-smelling chicken and rice dish Meagan prepared was tasty, and they shared a glass of red wine, which he brought. They also shared a bowl of vanilla ice cream with homemade chocolate syrup. They fed bites to each other. He lit the candles, and they moved to the couch where they had spent a significant portion of the past couple years together. They cuddled and kissed, not too serious though. They sat back quietly, contentedly holding hands until Marcus said, "I've been playing with a melody." That was not unusual. He asked, "Could I play part of it for you?"

"Certainly." She smiled and hid her disappointment that he was leaving her alone on the couch.

"Goes like this." He started picking a simple pattern, which lasted longer than normal. She wondered, *Why hasn't he started singing?* When he did, she thought, *He's emotional about this.* She chuckled inwardly as the first words filtered through the candlelit atmosphere.

> If I were a cat, I'd be purring
>
> If I were a dog, I'd be wagging my tail
>
> But since I am human, I'll just warm up my affections
>
> And let you know my love for you could never fail
>
> If I were younger, I'd be shy in your presence
>
> When I got old enough, I'd ask for a date
>
> But since I am the age I am and not getting younger

I'm happy that the love we share did not come too late

Because I love you

Would you like to share a house and a bed?

I love you

From the bottom of your feet to your head

I love you

I hope you're hearing what my heart says

"That's awesome, and so sweet," Meagan said. "And . . . ummm, what are you saying? Is there a hidden message in this song?" She was afraid to wonder, *Is this crazy boyfriend of mine finally hinting at a proposal? Can't be. Maybe. Maybe?*

Marcus set the guitar down. He rose to his feet and took those few steps over the cushy old carpet to the familiar couch. He thought, *She's so lovely and has been so incredibly patient with me.* She watched as he humbly knelt before her. Her heart skipped a beat as he pulled a miniature white container out of his pocket. She questioned whether she believed this was finally happening.

He held the small box in his left hand while he gently, and too slowly for Meagan, brought his right hand over and lifted the lid. The little case snapped open and lit up all on its own. Nestled inside the tiny, efficient compartment was its sole content, a ring. Sparkles from the solitaire diamond jubilantly traveled directly into Meagan's blue eyes, which were silently filling with understandable tears.

Marcus voiced the words he was at last able to form. From his humble position, both knees on the floor, he asked, "Will you marry me?"

They stood up. They hugged. They danced together. They laughed. They cried. They threw their hands up in praise, an expression they had picked up during the past year. Their hearts melded into a bond they knew they could never break.

Marcus said, "Well?"

"Well, what?"

"I don't think you said yes. Did you say yes? Did I miss that?"

"Yes! Yes, Mr. Marcus Paver, I will marry you! In a heartbeat! And with my whole heart. And here's a question for you: when?"

They chose a Sunday afternoon, October 9, 2033. They asked the pastor of their Sacramento church home to perform the service. They requested the chapel, which would be big enough but still intimate. Marcus reworked the purring and tail-wagging song from the night he proposed. It was a short engagement after a long courtship. Habakkuk Band members improvised a sweet version of the song with intricate acoustic picking, keyboard background, gentle djembe, inconspicuous percussion and perfect harmonies. They would sing. Marcus would not. Just before the wedding began the band joked about being "huh back-up band" for Marcus and his bride.

Darren and Rafa were invited, but neither showed. Rafa defended his need to decline. If there were any possibility that Darren might be there, it would be impossible for him to come. Darren didn't respond. Meagan and Marcus were sad, but not surprised. Radicalization had ended several friendships among people they knew.

Religious-i-zation, if it could be called that, also squelched a few relationships Marcus and Meagan cherished. They tried hard to stay in touch with these friends, but they were not about to compromise their newfound faith in Jesus.

A week before the wedding the two were finishing supper when Meagan brought up a question about a recent sermon they heard in church. "Jesus said, 'I did not come to bring peace, but a sword.' Do you think Jesus meant following Him might require cutting off some relationships, at least for a time? Your friend Chad from high school is an example. He's critical and antagonistic about anything that sounds religious in any way."

Marcus answered, "I think we have already unintentionally set boundaries. Sorry it has to be this way."

Meagan said, "Yeah. I'm sad some of our friends won't come to our wedding . . . but . . . Hey Marcus, let's get married anyway!" They both laughed, slid their chairs away from the table, stood and hugged each other tight. After a moment, Marcus leaned back so he could see her face. He smiled and said, "They couldn't keep me away if every one of them pulled a sword on me. I'm comin'!"

The day came and went. On the airplane headed for Cabo San Lukas, Mexico for their honeymoon, Meagan told Marcus, "It was the most beautiful day of my life. Our wedding was perfect. I love you so much, and I'm grateful for all our friends and family. The place was full of so much love." She was thoughtful for a moment before saying, "I think our relationship is deeper and stronger because we opened up to God's love. It seems like that's true for all kinds of relationships."

Marcus agreed.

Forty-Two

In contrast, neither Rafa's ultra-right-wingers nor Darren's lefties offered much true depth of relationship. Members on both sides bonded over their shared hatred of the other side. When one of their own took a hit on the battlefield, whether physical or verbal, they rallied around that one. They collectively intensified their profound distaste for the lost souls who had perpetrated that injustice against their compadres.

But true depth of empathy and compassion concerning the needs of others was being systematically weeded out of them, on both sides. It was necessary, on both sides.

The Solid Society, the right-wing group in which Rafa held membership, planned an early December rally. Rafa had been questioning his involvement with the group, but he decided to come as an observer.

The other side arrived to protest the protest, and Darren was among them. A popular right-wing speaker had flown in from Arizona. He excelled that night in rhetoric crafted to work up the fervor of the base.

Later, Rafa admitted he couldn't recall what issue was supposed to be the focus of the address that evening. By the late 2030s neither conservatives nor liberals spent much time trying to understand the nuances of the issues. They knew they hated the political positions of the opposite side. If they could silence them, America could be saved.

It was an unseasonably warm Friday evening, a pleasant night for a rally or an anti-rally rally. As was often the case, the protesters of the protest set up camp across the street. Contrary to the pleasant weather, an unpleasant and rowdy air permeated the gatherings on both sides. For more than a decade street protesting had gotten progressively more raucous and dangerous.

The Sacramento police were stationed nearby, but freedoms of speech and assembly restricted them from interfering unless violence broke out. They knew they could easily have their hands full of trouble and their vans full of detained protesters. The officers would have preferred to have been at home with their families for the start of the weekend.

As usual, which side took the first shot was unclear. What was staggering was how quickly the street became target practice for poorly trained vigilantes. The officers of the peace responded quickly, but not before the protesters fired a few bullets and catapulted a short salvo of rocks in both directions.

Darren was immediately caught up in the fray. He felt more than ready to defend his beliefs. He was unaware that his former friend was across the street. He might have assumed Rafa could be over there, but at this moment he was engrossed in the brief firefight. Rafa was there, not directly across, but only slightly askew to Darren's left, about forty yards away.

In the chaos of the dark and abrupt conflagration, and out of the corner of his eye, Rafa caught a glimpse of a shrouded figure. It crept out from behind a parked car. A dim yellowish beam from one of the streetlamps brought the face momentarily into focus. It was Darren. Without a doubt, it was him. The figure did not take careful aim. It pointed the gun across the street, toward the crowd. Darren pulled the trigger. Just one shot. Then the police rocketed tear gas canisters from their mortars. Darren was engulfed by the vaporous cloud, which drove an almost unbearable pain into his whole head. He stumbled away, along with the rest of the protesters.

Rafa heard the initial loud crack of that singular blast. The remainder of the sound faded off into a distant world. For Rafa, all the tactile evidences of the evening's unholy environment followed the reverberation of that little explosion off into the darkness. He fell into the stubbly, listless grass of the park that Sacramento's citizens had created for the enjoyment and relaxation of the general public.

The last phantasmagoria that reached his fading awareness was that of a young soldier plodding through vile-smelling smoke, a gas mask strapped around his face. The ghastly apparition would have fit nicely into a movie about any of the world wars. As he faded out of consciousness, Rafa caught a fleeting glimpse of the man's facial expression through the bulletproof glass bubble. It was a strained and saddened countenance in there.

The figure, which was a police officer, stopped, towering over Rafa who had just fallen into the green grass that now cradled a small but growing puddle of murky crimson liquid. He quickly peered down at the boy before scanning the vacating scene. A thought flitted through his head. *What a pity! These young lives. Wasted away! And they think they're saving America.*

Concerned about the possibility of more gunfire, the disgusted young officer took a second look around. The eerie, nearly deserted Sacramento park turned battlefield was now a dismal landscape dimly lit by its dismal, yellow-toned streetlamps. The officer was depressed by what he saw, in part because he was too fresh on the job to have developed a callousness to it all.

Suddenly, an unexpected interruption dragged his attention back to the situation at hand. A painful sounding cough and a deep moan drifted up from around his feet. He looked down. Only moments had passed since he had initially decided this still figure at his feet was dead.

He wasn't.

"Thank God!" the officer declared as he instantly dropped to the grass. The individual began to sit up, looked at the severe bleeding coming from his arm and lost consciousness again. The officer swiftly pulled a small portable gas mask from his pack and covered the man's face. He wrapped the arm with compresses and bandages.

The bullet, Darren's bullet, had entered Rafa's left arm exactly at the elbow, causing extensive damage to the intricate network of muscles, tendons, blood vasculature and bones inside. The intense pain had initially knocked him out. The unconscious boy, the puddle of blood, the gunshots, the whole warlike scene all added up to the appearance of one more senseless death in America's socio-political, uncivil war.

The figure began to regain consciousness, enough to make eye contact. The officer said, "You're gonna be okay. We're here to help." Rafa barely nodded, and the officer saw the fear in those eyes. "Listen, I'm calling 9-1-1 for you."

"This is Officer Terrence Blank with the Sacramento Police Department. I've got a man with a serious, but not life-threatening injury here at Howe Community Park. There's several ambulances here. Just send someone over to help me. I'm next to the parallel bars in the playground part of the park."

Returning his full attention to Rafa and hoping to be helpful, he said, "You're one lucky guy. You're alive! You could easily be dead.

God was watching out for you and let you live another day. The good Lord must have a job for you to do. I'd say about five inches over, and that bullet would've tore your heart open instead of your arm. But we'll get you outa here."

Since the chaos had mostly settled, Officer Blank chattered on. "You'd think we were in the Middle East, not an American park in central California." Rafa could not follow the man's words. His head was bouncing all over the place. The pain in his arm spread out to his shoulder and his head and was wreaking havoc with his nervous system. His thoughts were racing. *Darren did this! He used to be a friend. What kind of friend is that? What if they can't fix my arm? Or I can't play guitar again? Oh God, if there is a God. He's abandoned us along with this whole sorry planet.*

Forty-Three

Marcus understood Rafa's request when the text came. Rafa's family lived far away in Florida. "Yes, I can come. Is it Mercy General? I'm on my way." On the drive over, thoughts of Hunter all pin cushioned with needles and tubes bombarded his mind. He spoke out loud. *Same dang hospital! I don't wanna go there.* He attempted to turn his angst into prayer. "Help me, Lord Jesus. This is hard."

He spoke a text to Elijah and asked him to share with Habakkuk. He knew they would pray for God to guide him when he talked with Rafa. Though Marcus was still struggling with his heart-rending memories of Hunter, he pushed himself to focus on the present crisis. He hurried through the hospital hallways and found Rafa in an ICU cubicle.

"Darren shot me!" Rafa blurted out as soon as he saw Marcus. The words hung in the air. Rafa added, "Can you believe it?"

Marcus prayed under his breath. "Lord, help me be a witness to my friend. I can't do this alone."

"Oh Rafa, it's unbelievable, but thank God you're alive. Looks like we might've been planning another funeral."

Rafa said, "I hate Darren! What's my life gonna be like after what he's done to me? I know this, I'll find a way to make him pay for it." Marcus listened and tried to absorb a fraction of his friend's anguish. Rafa drifted in and out of consciousness because of the drugs administered to him.

When he was awake, he poured out his grief until he eventually said, "I'm out of it. Need to sleep. Surgery tomorrow morning."

Marcus promised, "I'll be back after work."

During the night and the next day on the way back to Mercy, Marcus searched for the best way to approach Rafa. He thought, *Words can be hard to find.*

He walked past the nurses' station, found the room and sat down. Before long, his friend revived from the anesthesia and pain meds. Marcus said, "Rafa, I hate seeing you like this. I'm praying for you, whether you want me to, or not. I know you're in pain, in more ways than one."

For most of that first hour Marcus spoke gently and did his best to comfort and encourage his old friend. Rafa seemed to appreciate it. His appreciation dissipated though when Marcus said, "But listen, I've been thinking about this. Is it really completely Darren's fault that this happened?"

Rafa was appalled by the question and spoke emphatically, "Yes, it is!"

"Wait, listen. Don't you have guns? Didn't you buy those guns so you could join in this horrible war that's going on? Weren't you doing basically the same thing Darren was doing last night? Why is it all his fault?"

Rafa didn't answer. Marcus couldn't tell if his friend had clammed up in anger, passed out again, or if he was thinking about what had just been said.

A couple minutes passed before Marcus asked, "Are you there?"

Rafa sounded frustrated as he answered, "Yes."

Slowly, carefully and prayerfully, Marcus went on. "I learned this verse. It's from the Bible. It says we've all sinned, and we all fall short of the glory of God. Maybe the way we turn our streets and parks into violent combat zones is not the fault of just one person. Maybe it's the result of the sinfulness in all of us. We let hatred take over. We ignore God's teachings, and we ignore the presence of God. Maybe all this trouble is part my fault. And maybe part your fault, too, Rafa."

Marcus paused a moment, then said, "Hunter found out something, and I've discovered it too. God is here, with us in the world we live in. God has answers that this world can't give us."

Rafa remained silent. Marcus waited and prayed under his breath. The emergency room machines kept up their intermittent beeping. A doctor spoke in hushed tones with a family out in the hall. Enough time passed that Marcus began to wonder if his friend had dozed off again. He leaned forward, thinking he might hear Rafa snoring quietly, but Rafa opened his eyes. He stared directly at Marcus, a serious look on his face, almost pleading.

He said, "I need something, something better than what I've got, better than what my life has become. I've been consumed with anger. It started when Hunter died, when I took Piper up to see him. It was terrible to see him all hooked up to those machines." He glanced over at the heart monitor beside the bed and continued. "Such an unbearable hatred took root inside me. I wanted to lash out. At something. At someone. At anything. I had to do something. Anything. It's hurting me. It's killing me."

He closed his eyes for a long moment. He opened them, looked away from Marcus, and said, "You're probably right, about me having sins in my life too, like everybody else, but it's hard to think about that." Rafa breathed deeply. "And it's impossible to do anything but blame Darren." He brought his eyes back to Marcus. "I can't help but blame him. He shot me." With a painful look he added, "But you're right, I shouldn't have been out there. Something needs to change. Something needs to change in me."

Marcus didn't rush in. He waited. He prayed. He waited for a leading from the Spirit. When it seemed right, he told Rafa, "Here's the starting point; it's a prayer: 'Dear God, I'm a sinner. I've done wrong. I can't fix myself. God, You made me. I need You to make me over again. Help me make the changes I need to make. I want You, Lord Jesus in my life. You're a fixer. You're a transformer. You're a Friend who loves and teaches us how to love. Lord Jesus, come into my heart.'"

Silence again.

Finally, Rafa spoke, clearly struggling. "Marcus, help me. I can't do this. I don't know how." Silence, then, "I shouldn't say I hate God, but I'm mad at God. He let all this happen. Hunter's death was senseless. God lets so many people die meaningless deaths. And look at my arm! I can't stop myself from hating Darren. Why doesn't God stop all this, if He's so powerful?"

"It's because we're not puppets," was Marcus' response. "Do you see that, Rafa? If God manipulated all our actions, He wouldn't have children. He'd have robots. God wants children who choose to love Him, and whom He can love."

Marcus paused and let Rafa think. Then he said, "We can choose evil. We can constantly mistreat other people. Or we can choose truth, humility and love. Jesus taught the craziest, amazing thing. He said, 'Love your enemies.' Hard to do, obviously, but it's a world changer.

"Rafa, let Him into your heart. He can change you; He can change anyone, and it's always for the better. If it isn't better, it isn't God."

"Okay, Marcus, thanks. You're a good friend, but I'm sorry, I'm getting tired. I'll think about what you said." Marcus asked if he could do anything for his friend.

Rafa said, "No, the nurses are here."

As Marcus walked through the sliding glass doors onto the sidewalk, he realized the sun had already gone down. His footsteps seemed heavy as he walked through the partially lit parking lot past his car. He kept walking until he was out from under the canopy of artificial lights. In the natural darkness he peered up through the scattered clouds to the stars, which seemed dim, not brilliant like they appear up in the mountains. He prayed, "God, You made the stars. You made us. We need some remaking down here. I do. Rafa and Darren do. I'm so glad You made a way for my buddy Hunter to get to Heaven. Sounds like You make room for everybody who believes. Help me help my friends believe."

Forty-Four

Marcus dreaded punching the contact icon to make the grim call he knew he had to make. Still unsure, he punched, and it rang. "Darren, can we meet? I need to talk with you."

Darren asked, "Whada ya wanna talk about?"

Marcus replied, "I'd rather sit down together. The phone doesn't seem right this time. It's pretty serious."

Darren said, "I'm not in a very good mood."

Marcus prayed under his breath. "Lord, I need your help here." He decided to say, "We're both going to want lunch. None of us have gotten rich, not yet anyway. But I got paid, and I'd like to buy. I can take a break from work around 1:00 and meet you at the Yard House, downtown."

After an extended silence, "Alright, if you insist." The tone made it clear that Darren wasn't happy about it. Marcus considered that maybe Darren wasn't happy about much of anything these days.

Marcus said, "See you there" before he saw that the call had already ended. "Lord," he prayed, "this is not going to be easy, but I have to tell him."

Darren slouched in through the glass door of the coffee shop. He looked unkempt, unshaven, unhappy with a scowl that may have taken up permanent residence on his cheerless face. Marcus sensed an oppression, a spiritual darkness as his old friend slithered into the booth.

Darren said, "So what is it you just have to talk about?"

Marcus thought, *Where's my long lost friend? He hasn't shown up, at least not yet.* He said, "Darren, we'll get to the main subject. Let's do a little catchin' up first. It's been a while."

Darren responded sullenly, "Okay," as he peered back across. Marcus found himself grappling for a topic beyond small talk but innocuous enough to prevent a stormy eruption from the other side of the booth.

"I don't know, Darren. What's been goin' on with you?"

His response of, "Not much" was accompanied with a blank stare.

It appeared to Marcus that small talk might be worse than pulling teeth. So, he said, "Okay, I'll get to the point then. Rafa believes that you fired the shot that hit him last night. He was at that Solid Society rally. He's not dead. He could've been. He's seriously injured."

Darren continued to stare as he internalized the initial shock of this news. Marcus thought it looked like his old friend was mentally steeling himself. *He thinks of himself as a soldier in a war.*

Apparently concerned about his own wellbeing, Darren probed, "Did he go to the police with this phony theory?"

Marcus replied, "No, he's not gone to the police, not as far as I know. But he seems one hundred percent sure that the bullet that hit him came from your gun. He said you came out from behind a parked car just before you fired."

"Guess I need to practice my aim," Darren callously responded.

Marcus said, "I'm not the judge, but Darren, I have to ask, are you not the least bit concerned that you may have seriously wounded an old friend of yours?"

Darren answered, "It's his own fault. I've said it before; he's chosen to be on the wrong side of history. And if that's all you wanted to tell me, I'm outta here."

Marcus kept his gaze positioned on Darren's face while he prayed silently. "Now what do I do?" Marcus Paver knew he needed to take another step forward in spite of his uncertainty. He had to trust God for a leading.

He said, "Darren, are you sure, are you confident in yourself about the direction your life is headed?"

Darren interrupted. "Well, listen to you, Mr. righteous, Mr. self-righteous Christian man. Whadda you know? Whadda you know about my life and the world I live in? You hide out in your little churches and your Christian band, and you let the whole world go to crap."

Marcus had to respond. "Really, Darren? Really? You think you're making the world a better place? A friend of yours is in surgery today, and it's the same hospital where they unplugged Hunter. Rafa may never use his arm again, and it's almost certain that your decision to pull that trigger put him there. Forgive me if I'm wrong, but I can't see an ounce of concern coming from you."

"Like I said, I'm outta here" were the last words Darren uttered before he stood up. He glared down at Marcus, cursed him and said, "And stay out of my life, you religious scumbag."

It took Marcus a couple minutes before he recovered enough to jokingly inform himself, "Well, I guess that didn't go exactly as planned." Soon the waitress returned. "Would you like to order, or wait for your friend? Is he coming back?"

Marcus gazed out the window and uttered, "Yeah, he's coming back. Someday. Not for lunch today, but he's gotta come back, yeah." Marcus glanced at the nice-looking waitress, then back out the window. He thought, *That's what the Habakkuk boys call a faith declaration.* The waitress waited, feeling puzzled about her customer. Finally, he looked down at the menu and said, "I'd like, let's see, how about the pepper jack burger. And, yeah, sweet potato fries. By the way, how's your day going?"

"Well, kinda crumby, if you really want to know. My boyfriend left me yesterday. So, it's not easy."

Marcus expressed his sympathy with his face, then said, "Seems like nobody's life is easy. Maybe he'll come back. Would it be good if he came back?"

She said, "Definitely. He's a good guy."

Marcus said, "Then I hope he comes back. I'll even pray. Would you send up a prayer that my friend, the one that just left, will come back to his senses?"

"That's what my boyfriend needs to do, come back to his senses. I don't know much about praying, but I could try."

Marcus said, "Thank you."

She said, "No, thank you!"

He finished his burger and sweet potato fries and stepped out into a cloudy and breezy December afternoon. *Brrr. Turned cold! Where did that warmer weather disappear to? And where'd my friends go? Who kidnapped the real Darren? Talk about cold!*

Forty-Five

Meagan asked Marcus what he wanted for Christmas. He answered, "I want my friends back."

She said, "I'll see what I can do," and she did what she could do. She took her husband's heartache to the Father. She asked God to intervene in Rafa's and Darren's lives. She prayed that God would work through her husband. She prayed and didn't give up.

Winter phased into spring. With the warmer weather, an alliance of nine area churches planned a large outdoor rally. They invited Habakkuk Band to play. The organizers were aware of the band's growing following throughout the area. Elijah and Marcus were writing songs that spoke prophetically of the power of God to change people's hearts and thus change society. The band and Marcus had gelled together beautifully.

For the rally Habakkuk Band was the backup band. They joked about living up to their name. A singer with a decent-sized national fan base and increasing airplay had also been contracted to come. Appreciation for both the national artist and the local band brought out more than a thousand lovers of spiritual music.

Habakkuk Band had grown extremely effective at covering the latest, well-loved songs of praise and worship. People often told them that they liked the Habakkuk versions better than the originals. As they played, they stepped into the glorious presence of the King, and the people followed them in. That night they ended their set with an original that fit the troubled times. Marcus took a minute to explain the origin of the song.

"I had a dream. Like when I was asleep. A young woman was being attacked by evil. The exact nature of the evil was unclear, but she was in danger. Then, mysteriously, inexplicably, a strong voice came from above and beyond her. As she struggled alone in the darkness, she heard this: 'To the powers of evil she'll rise up and say, be gone, for Jesus is living in me.'

"I woke in the middle of the night with that dream, and I thought, *that one line had a rhythm to it.* Is this crazy? But listen.

> To the powers of evil
> She'll rise up and say
> Be gone
> For Jesus is living in me

Feel the beat? Here's the song."

Habakkuk's super cool drummer played the first three measures alone. Then the guitar, bass and keys dropped in. Marcus sang the lead.

> As darkness grows darker, she longs to stand strong
> With wickedness closer, she searches for her song
> Then a voice comes from somewhere
> And speaks in her ear
> The words of her courage that she needs to hear

To the powers of evil she'll rise up and say,

"Be gone, for Jesus is living in me."

In a world that's gone crazy she starts to lose heart

But the light that's inside her will never go out

A voice comes from somewhere and speaks in her ear

The words of her courage that she needs to hear

To the powers of evil she'll rise up and say,

"Be gone, for Jesus is living in me."

After the song, Elijah stepped up to his mic. "People, the darkness has become oppressive. Let's not be oppressed, not in any way. We are overcomers, 'more than conquerors through Him who loved us.' 'Greater is He that is in us than he that is in the world.' Push it back! Push back the darkness that's all around us and inside us. Rise up and say, 'Be gone. Jesus is living in me.'" A solid cheer rose up from the crowd. Marcus thought, *Whether we cheer or not, the Holy Spirit is in this!*

The band exited via the corrugated metal steps on the side of the platform. Marcus decided to search out a different perspective on the stage, a spot where he could enjoy watching and listening to the headliner band. He strolled past the rows of white folding chairs on the field and the people of all ages who filled them. He found an open space along a back wall and leaned up against it.

After a few minutes he glanced to his left. He took a second look, and exclaimed, *That's Rafa. He's here!* If Marcus had had any doubt about who it was, the sling on the left arm drove that doubt away. Marcus walked toward him thinking, *This grin on my face could light up the whole stadium!* Rafa smiled weakly, but the smile was overtaken by a worried look.

Over the substantial loudness of the music, Marcus almost shouted, "You're here! Thank you for coming. How did you like Habakkuk Band? Hey, let's get outside the fence where we can hear each other." They walked through the gate without words. They stopped and faced each other, and Marcus asked, "How're you doing?" Rafa quickly looked away, but not before Marcus saw the tracks of tears engraved on his old friend's face.

Marcus probed. "Rafa, I think I saw a tear there." Rafa looked down at his feet and then at his useless left arm. Marcus said, "It's okay, I've shed lots of 'em over the past couple years. We all have. I don't know for sure, but I'm guessing this might be a different kind of tear, the kind that comes when something important is happening to us."

Rafa took a deep breath, lifted his head to look Marcus in the eye and replied, "I'm not sure what's happening to me." He hesitated and looked down at his feet and his arm again. He seemed unsure, broken, lost. "Marcus, I know you have something I don't have. Hunter had it. And Piper. Maybe I need what you have. I know you would say it has something to do with God."

Marcus replied, "It has a lot to do with God. I obviously don't know everything about God; I'm just learning. But I'll help if I can."

Rafa said, "Thanks."

Marcus said, "There is one thing I could do right now. Would you let me pray for you?"

Rafa looked down, shook his head slowly from side to side and said, "Sure. Go ahead. Can't hurt." Then he looked up with a Hunter-style quizzical face and asked, "It won't hurt, will it?"

Marcus smiled and said, "It will hurt. But it's such a good hurt. It will hurt deep down in your heart, but it will set you free, really free. When somebody believes in Jesus, he begins to die to his selfish desires. That's not easy, but it leads to something that is so good."

Without even looking religious, Marcus started talking to God. "Lord, we need You. We all do." Marcus put his left hand on Rafa's right shoulder and his right hand gently on the sling on Rafa's left arm. "Thank You, Lord for touching this friend of mine. I pray send your Holy Spirit and your healing power down on him. Right now!"

"Rafa, God wants to help you. He can give you a peace you'll never find in a world that rejects God and the truth about life."

Rafa's face took on a pensive appearance. Marcus waited. Then Rafa told Marcus, "That song you wrote and shared just now, it spoke to me. I think there's some kind of darkness in me. I don't know how to get rid of it. It's killing me."

Marcus quoted the song. "She'll rise up and say, 'Be gone, for Jesus is living in me.' She can say that because the power of Jesus' Spirit is living in her. You can have that same Spirit, the Holy Spirit, the Spirit of power living in you. But you have to ask. Jesus will give you the help you need, same help that I need. Jesus called Himself 'the Light of the world,' and He said that light overcomes darkness. That is always true in the physical world. It's true in the spiritual world, too. Rafa, just do it. Let the light of Jesus, the light of God come into your heart."

The music continued from the stage. Rafa listened to the applause after the band finished another song. Only a few stadium lights were lit. When Rafa looked through the gate, he saw hands lifted above the crowd and thought the scene had a mystical appearance. He wondered if he would ever lift his arm without that horrible pain. He and Marcus stood outside the camp of worshippers, but the mood, the spirit and the feeling all splashed over the fence and touched them.

Still feeling lost, Rafa gazed at this friend who had always been one of the kindest people he knew. He remembered how Marcus had embraced him so generously into their old band. He thought of his beloved Alvarez acoustic he couldn't play anymore, and he felt the sting of regret. Even so, standing there just outside the rally, the Holy Spirit touched him. His mental objections began to melt away. His emotional hardness softened, and he decided to let his pain take a backseat.

His friend said, "Rafa, just say this, 'Lord Jesus, come into my heart,'" and Rafa said it out loud. "Say, 'Forgive me of all my sins, and fill me with the Holy Spirit.'" And Rafa's life fell into a new trajectory, one that was headed for eternal life, and not unending darkness. What the two of them did not know was that Darren, shrouded in the dark shadows, was watching them.

Forty-Six

That night at the rally, four months after he had pulled the trigger, Darren saw firsthand the damage he had caused. In self-defense, he continued to tell himself that no one knew for sure, or had proof, that it was his bullet that hit Rafa. He had heard nothing from the police.

Yet when honest with himself, he had to admit that it was unlikely that Rafa would concoct a story like that. He also knew Marcus was sharp enough to catch it if Rafa had been lying about it. In addition, Rafa had accurately described to Marcus the scene from four months earlier. As Rafa said, Darren had snuck out from behind a parked car and took that shot. How would he know that kind of detail if he hadn't seen it?

Darren was affected by this first look at a former friend, now a guitarist with one entirely incapacitated arm. He was far enough away to be unseen. Yet across that gap he perceived the pain in Rafa's face. He observed the discouragement and downtrodden appearance of a guy who was once cheerful, fully alive, friendly, and an excellent musician.

A hairline crack emerged in Darren's emotional armor that night. The resulting feelings were scary enough that he yearned to bury them or bolt far away. But he was stuck with the uncomfortable weight of his own poor choices, and that convicting heaviness began to seep through the tiny fracture.

A week passed before one evening Marcus looked at his phone and thought, *really? Can this be?* He tapped the button and said with a question mark in his voice, "Darren?" A thought blinked through his mind; maybe someone stole Darren's phone. Or worse, *he's been killed, and one of his friends is using his phone to let people know.*

Nope. It was him.

"I was at your rally. I don't believe all that Christian crap, but I saw you talkin' with Rafa. I've always wished he hadn't gotten sucked into all that conservative nonsense, but" —Darren searched for his words— "It looks like he's hurting. He used to be a friend."

"Yeah," Marcus replied. "Our lives sure took a bad turn."

He heard Darren take a deep breath and exhale slowly. He apparently had to force the next words out of his throat. "Do you think I shot him?"

The question hung in the air for a long moment. Then Marcus answered the question. "Yes, I do."

Darren asked, "Why didn't you go to the police with it?"

Fighting with his long-held frustration, Marcus tried to explain his complicated mindset. "It's a war. You both think you're in a war. So sad that it's against each other. Not everyone, including the police, would see it this way, but it's a microcosm of the way the world is. We choose sides and shoot at each other. I suppose that sounds simplistic, but you both armed yourselves and enlisted. On opposite sides."

Darren's response started out harsh, but then mellowed. "I believe what I believe; and that's not going to change. But Marcus, believe me. It wasn't. No, never. Never was it my intention to hurt Rafa."

Marcus said, "Maybe we should start thinking about such things before we start pulling triggers."

Darren answered, "You don't understand. You got your rosy worldview, and you think all these problems are gonna fix themselves. They aren't."

Marcus said, "I don't think problems fix themselves. People do, and people who seek God's help seem to become better fixers. People who are quick to kill others because of their political beliefs—well, they just dig a deeper hole."

"You don't know anything, Marcus."

Marcus responded, "I know I have more peace in my life than you do. You could have more peace."

Darren's voice sounded sarcastic. "Right. And I suppose that has something to do with God."

Marcus answered, "You're right about that. God made us and knows how we tick."

Darren stated, "I don't believe in God."

Marcus said, "I know you don't. But if you'd look around, take a look at what God made—if you'd pay attention to the lifechanging experiences of people who do believe in God—you'd see things you haven't seen. I think you will someday."

Darren said, "I doubt it."

Marcus smiled, winked at his phone and spoke into it. "That's your problem, old friend. Doubt." He let that hang for a moment. "And I doubt—there's that word again—that you're ever going to find peace in your life without serious change. I'm not saying I don't need change; I do. But the first change, the most far-reaching, is to stop running from God."

Darren responded, "Okay, and thanks for nothing." And he was gone.

Marcus looked upward and said, "God, I know You're big enough. You're not going to disappear because my friend's heart is so cold right now."

Marcus remembered a story Elijah had shared a few weeks earlier. A vicious street fighter, a woman in the Sacramento area had renounced her radicalism and was now living a different life.

Marcus thought, *If she can change, so can Darren.* He prayed, "Lord, help me never give up on my friend."

Forty-Seven

Her name was Livvy. She and Darren were acquainted, having both been assigned to Training Unit 26 with the Local Liberties League. They sat together at a few coaching sessions and arrived simultaneously at the League's shooting range a couple times. After that first chance meeting, they visited out on the sidewalk. The warm afternoon sunshine with a gentle spring breeze enhanced a pleasant conversation. Both left with a feeling of respect and admiration for each other's priorities.

After their second encounter at the range, Darren suggested, "How about going for a drink? I like The Spot on Stockton Boulevard."

She said, "Sure."

They took seats at the bar and ordered beers. Darren said, "You told me you finished college. Whacha been doin' since then?"

She replied, "I started with the merchant marines and stayed longer than expected. I traveled around the world! Now I'm driving a forklift. My political science major isn't making me rich, but I'm available to work with the league, and I count that as important."

Darren chuckled and said, "My degree in political theory hasn't turned out to be too lucrative either, but we need to help turn this country in a better direction."

She said, "That's so right, Darren. Those conservative crazies out there might mess everything up if we let them. It's good to associate with people who think alike. It's hard when you have to distance yourself from your own family members."

Darren asked, "Have you had to do that, Livvy."

She said, "Yes, with some of them."

He said, "That's hard."

They finished their beers, went their ways and didn't talk for most of a month.

"Darren, did you hear about Livvy?" It was another league member on the phone.

"No, I haven't. Why? What's up?"

The guy went on. "She has un-enlisted herself from the League."

Darren said, "You're kidding. Why would she do that?"

He answered, "Don't know, but someone said it had something to do with religion. Who knows?"

Darren ended the call and told himself, *I need a firsthand account of this.* When Livy answered the phone he said, "Yup, it's me. I'm gonna miss you at the League. What happened?"

She responded, "It's a long story."

He said, "Well, I'd like to hear the whole thing. Can we get together?"

She answered slowly. "Well, I don't know."

He said, "Please. I'm really curious."

Livvy asked, "Will you promise to be patient with me?"

He said, "I promise."

"Okay then," and she suggested The Spot on Stockton.

She ordered pot stickers and Vietnamese coffee. He asked for a Modelo, which they had, and chips and salsa, which they did not have. So, he got pot stickers. Livvy silently asked herself, *how do I explain this to someone who doesn't know me that well?*

She said, "Darren, I'm not sure where to start. I'm glad you're interested, I really am, but this isn't easy."

Darren said. "I'm a learner. I like to catch all the details. So, tell me, and help me understand."

Livvy tentatively responded, "You'll probably hate me when I do."

Darren looked truly puzzled and asked, "Livvy, what have you done? I can't imagine you doing anything so terrible that I could hate you for it. How could anybody hate you? That's crazy."

She said, "Well, Darren, when I've told people, especially members of the League, the responses have not been positive. Nobody's told me to my face that they hate me, but they have treated me hatefully and shunned me."

Darren's face reflected his perplexed reaction to what she just shared. Silently, he racked his brain for an inkling of what she could have done. He asked himself silly questions. *Did she murder her grandmother? Rob a convenience store?* He tried to think more serious. *She's a capable fighter and a proven sharpshooter. Maybe she had to snuff out some conservative clod, and she's beating herself up about it."* His mind drifted away until her voice broke through and pulled his attention back to their booth at The Spot. He looked across the white vinyl-topped table at Livvy.

She said, "I've become a Christian believer. I don't think the policies and attitude of the League fit the life of a person who wants to live for Christ."

Darren frowned and blew his breath out over his bottom lip. He stared at her in disbelief. After a moment, he thought, *Darn it! They got another one, stole another one of my friends. When's this gonna stop?*

Livvy said, "So, Darren. You can turn your back on me right now. If that's what you have to do, do it. I'm getting used to it."

He said, "Livvy, I just don't get it. We have a cause, a reason to fight for the kind of world we want to live in."

She replied, "Are we really, is the League really makin' the world a better place? Moms are afraid to take their kids out in public, afraid they'll get shot. I have not abandoned my progressive ideology or my passion to protect the rights of disenfranchised people. But I've found a better way to go about it. It's a way that is based in love, truth and grace, more than in rigid hatred of half the country because they think differently than I do."

Darren broke in, "So you think these conservative crazies are not ruining our country?"

Her face took on an intense appearance when she said, "Darren, there is a power much more sinister than conservative-thinking people. It's a dark power. It's behind the scenes. It captures gentle people's minds and turns them into killers. It's not right. There's a battle going on, a spiritual one. I've left the League, and I've joined a better army. I have a new leader, and it's Jesus. I plan to follow His commands now. One of those commands is that I love my enemies. It's pretty hard to love them while you're simultaneously in training to turn the quiet streets of your own community into a battlefield."

Darren realized he was getting a headache. These recent assaults against his heartfelt commitment to his cause had started chipping away at his belief system. Something foreign and strange was beginning to seep through that recent crack in his armor. Beyond his comprehension, that alien feeling presented itself as being somehow right. He struggled with an emerging desire to open that fracture a little wider and let more of this mysterious thing find its way into his head and even deeper.

I have to snap out of this, he told himself.

His face suddenly hardened. Livvy saw it coming and grieved over what she knew she was about to hear.

Darren spoke sternly and seriously. "Get outta here, Livvy! I've had enough of this."

Livvy did not move.

She was a fighter and was willing to stay and fight for the soul of a new friend whom she knew was grossly misled. "Darren, why? Why are you so angry?"

He started to rise but was suddenly shaky. He couldn't understand why he couldn't drag himself away from Livvy. He turned his face toward the door but began to slip backwards, back into the booth. He laid a hand on the table to steady himself. It felt like an unseen cord had snagged him and was too powerful to overcome. So, he gave in and sat there, confused, frustrated, angry. He closed his eyes.

A few moments of silence passed before he felt her hand on his. Whether to recoil or welcome the uninvited touch, he didn't know which. He opened his eyes and beheld the almost angelic face of compassion from the other side of the table. Unexplained tears began to well up in his eyes. And in hers. Still neither spoke. Their waiter began to approach the table but turned away. The sounds of conversation, clinking plates and music from the sound system all faded into a distant world, far away from the one they shared in that moment.

He made himself talk to Livvy. "I don't understand why I'm so angry. I wanna figure it out." The angelic face morphed into the gracious smile of a friend who refused to walk away.

Forty-Eight

"Have you heard the news?" It was Rafa, sounding urgent. Marcus hadn't. "Bring it up on your phone. Russia's attacking Europe. They're calling it 'tactical.' It's possible a hundred thousand may have already been killed. We're involved because we're the weapons supplier. You knew that. It's scary."

"Oh no!" was Marcus' guttural response as he joined his friend along with populations all over the world in mentally processing the profoundly disturbing news. That old phrase from high school sociology class popped up again: "man's inhumanity to man."

Marcus spoke into his phone, talking to himself as much as to Rafa. "We always learn to hate, don't we? We don't learn to love our enemies like Jesus said. We kill millions of innocent people and call it 'collateral damage.' We think we've done the right thing. The people of Russia and Ukraine are still reeling from the hundreds of thousands killed back in the 20s. They are incapable of forgiving and reconciling."

Then not out loud to Rafa, but to himself Marcus said, *No surprise. Look at me; I can't even get my two friends to forgive and reconcile. Rafa lost an arm; we could lose the planet!*

Sharing the deep concern of people around the world, Marcus and his friends watched and waited, and some prayed. Each day for the next few weeks the conflagration remained contained to the areas where it started. Ukraine had immediately fired back that first day and repaid Russia for their first strike. Pressure from the international community had prevented both sides from launching any more "tactical" nuclear missiles.

During those first few weeks Marcus was constantly focused on news from the Euro-Russian War. Eventually, he realized his attention was beginning to taper off. His phone rang, and the name showed up. He could not mask his surprise. He asked, "Darren? Is this you?"

"Yeah. I need to talk."

"Okay. I'm good with that."

As Darren began, Marcus thought he sounded less arrogant than he had in a long time. Darren said, "I've been looking around, and I see what's happening in the world. It's gotten so messed up."

Marcus replied, "That's for sure."

Darren went on, "I'm concerned along with everybody else about what's happening on the other side of the globe, but my trouble right now hits closer to home. I can't shake the feeling that I've helped to make this mess. You know, the war, the potential World War Three, that's one thing. But the mess starts at lower levels, doesn't it?"

Marcus responded, "Good insight!"

Darren continued, "So, for me it's not only Europe and Russia; it's Sacramento. I've made my town a more violent place. We lost Hunter because there were people out there who thought their political opponents had to be silenced. I got caught up in the same mindset. Europe is devastated, but so is Sacramento. There's so much heartache."

"I'm with you, Darren. It's disheartening and scary."

"Listen, Marcus. I can't do anything about Europe, but maybe I can patch something up here." The phone went silent. Marcus waited.

Darren came back in a broken voice. "I hurt Rafa. Badly. Now it's hurting me. I can't sleep. I'm worried all the time. I need to make a change. I've thought this over for a long time." Darren hesitated and then asked, "Do you think Rafa would be willing to talk with me?"

Marcus was amazed by what he just heard, even more so by Darren's next question. "And could you set that up?"

Marcus thought, *Set that up? Uhh, how do you do that? Are we asking for a miracle here?* The phone remained quiet while Marcus' mind raced. *Am I supposed to speak to this storm? There's certainly been a storm of trouble between these two. But I've wanted to calm storms for most of my life.*

Darren asked, "You there?"

Marcus snapped back to the present. "Yeah, I'm here. But do you know what you're asking for, Darren? I don't know if Rafa could handle it. Losing the use of that arm . . . I think you can imagine how hard, how terrible that has been for him."

Darren's response was guttural, "Awwgh, Marcus, I am so sorry. I was so wrong, so misled, so confused, so angry with the world. And I made the world a nastier place because I was angry. I could have, and I should have dealt with Hunter's death better than I did. I turned it into revenge that made no sense."

Marcus responded, "None of us handled Hunter's passing well. Can you give me a minute to think about getting you and Rafa together?"

Darren said, "Yeah, sure."

Marcus struggled, thinking, *I've prayed I'd get my friends back. Maybe this is it. Sounds impossible, but who knows? Lord, please guide me.*

The phone stayed quiet.

Marcus finally, hesitatingly said, "Okay, I'll try to communicate with Rafa. We'll see what happens. Maybe I can convey to him how badly you feel."

Darren quietly responded. "Thank you."

"And, Darren, I'm going to pray for you."

The hesitation wasn't long before Darren answered. "I want you to pray for me." Marcus thought, *that's new.*

Darren admitted, "I need help."

Marcus said, "Yeah, we all do. And you know I found help when I turned to God."

It took a moment before Darren said, "Yeah, I see that. It must make you feel better."

Marcus said, "Yes, and that's because it's real. Some people think it's just a fairytale that makes people feel better when they hear it. But that wouldn't last. This does. When a person discovers and believes the truth about life and why we're here, it changes us deep down inside, for the long haul. And, yeah, it feels good."

Darren said, "Well, let me know what you find out from Rafa."

Marcus began to speak but realized Darren was gone.

Marcus made the call later that day. "Rafa, how's it goin' for you?"

"Not too bad . . . for a one-armed guitar picker. Thanks for asking." Rafa was quiet for a moment, then in a tone dripping with sarcasm, "Maybe I'll learn to pick with my toes. Wouldn't that be impressive?" Marcus quietly soaked in his friend's heartache. Rafa continued, "But, really, thanks for asking. I'm makin' a little progress. Therapy's helping, both physical and the other kind."

Marcus felt a heavy weight on his shoulders. He almost abandoned the underlying purpose of the call, then decided the window of opportunity might pass. He prayed silently. "Lord, help! I can't handle this without You."

He breathed deeply before he said, "Rafa, I received a call yesterday. I never imagined I'd get one like that."

Rafa's voice sounded cautious. "Oh yeah? Who was it?"

Marcus hated to say the name. "It was Darren."

Rafa didn't speak, but Marcus heard a long, deep sigh.

"He wants to talk with you."

Rafa immediately said, "No!"

Marcus' natural first thought was that Rafa was dead set against talking with Darren, but he tried to hope for another possibility. *Maybe he meant, "No, as in, 'No, I can't believe it!'"* Marcus did his best to believe that a miracle could happen. He knew it would take an act from God for Rafa to agree to talk with Darren.

Marcus said, "I doubted that we would ever see this, but Darren sounded desperately distraught over what he did to you."

Rafa spoke emphatically. "He should!"

Marcus said, "He does, and this was surprising. I offered to pray for him, and he wanted me to pray. I think he's beginning to take responsibility for what he did to you. He's like . . . repentant. The war overseas has affected him, but he's tired of the one here at home, too. But you know Darren, he's kind of hard to read sometimes."

Rafa quickly responded. "You got that right!"

Even though Rafa's words were predictably noncommittal up to this point, still Marcus sensed the Holy Spirit working. He knew Rafa had been attending a home group and that his faith was growing.

Marcus heard Rafa take a deep breath before he said, "I'll think about it."

"Thanks, Rafa."

Off the phone, Marcus prayed. "Lord, this is amazing. It could happen, that is, if You're still working miracles down here."

Forty-Nine

Rafa let Marcus know he would be willing to talk.

Darren said he was ready, but with a condition. "I'm not about to open the door for him to pay me back, Marcus. When we come to the meeting place, you need to frisk both of us."

Marcus brought that news to Rafa, who blurted out, "Sounds like he can shoot in the dark, but he's chicken to go face to face with his target."

Marcus pleaded, "Let's not turn this into a duel. Darren sounded entirely sincere when I talked with him. He doesn't want to hurt you more than what he's already done. When he learned he shot you, he was devastated, not at first, but when he had time to think it over. Are you going to turn this into revenge?"

Slowly Rafa answered. "No. I won't." Picking up the pace he said, "You'd better worry about your friend Darren, the dangerous one, not me."

Marcus suggested they meet at the university and walk along Putah Creek trail. Both agreed with the plan. Darren and Marcus would arrive first, park and walk forty yards beyond the trailhead where Darren would submit to a thorough frisking. Marcus would call Rafa and let him know they were ready for him.

The trees along the creek had passed the budding stage and had sprouted spring leaves in various shades of green. A light breeze with the sun appearing now and then through the partly cloudy sky made it a congenial day. The standard variety of spring birds and their young flitted from branch to branch and chirped their sporadic melodies. From where Darren and his mediator stood, they could see the top stories of the school of medicine. Both silently remembered happier days on this campus.

Rafa did not show on time. They waited. Darren kept shifting his weight back and forth and rapidly tapping one foot then the other. Marcus kept frowning and staring back at the parking lot.

Finally, Darren announced, "There he is."

Rafa appeared apprehensive as he approached slowly through the mostly empty parking lot. His left arm hung helpless in its black sling. He stopped at the trailhead beside a large, flowing oak tree and looked like he might decide to duck behind it for protection. Darren stood still, hardly moving a muscle, except that his eye started to twitch. Marcus forced himself to walk over to perform the second frisking. He hoped no one would drive by. As he approached Rafa, he thought, *Why? Why have we come to this? We used to be friends.*

The two started to walk slowly toward Darren, who looked sheepish and broken. Marcus thought, *He's not looking like he thinks he runs the world anymore.*

Rafa was broken in his own way, having now spent half a year battling the depression that naturally accompanied the mindboggling limitations caused by one pull of a trigger. Still thirty yards away, he gazed at Darren, and his thoughts and emotions traveled off in a hundred directions. The hatred was there. So was the relentless physical and emotional pain and the despondency caused by the loss.

Another ten yards closer, an unexpected feeling caught Rafa off-guard. He thought, *I can't believe this, but I feel pity. I actually feel sorry for this wimp who destroyed my arm.*

He kept walking slowly beside Marcus while a disturbing memory took over his mind. He was at that other rally and felt that girl's pain as his rock smashed into her face. He saw the blood spurt from her split nose and sliced forehead and drip from her chin to the dirt. The image haunted him nearly every day, except that it was often overshadowed by his hatred for Darren.

Rafa asked himself, *I wonder if Darren has ever been troubled by what he did to me. Right now he looks humble.*

Only ten more yards to go and Rafa realized how much his new-found faith had changed him. He thought, *I've experienced more healing in my emotions than I thought possible. I would never have made progress like this if I hadn't received Christ into my life. This is hard to imagine, but maybe Darren will accept Christ and be changed. He doesn't deserve it, but neither do I.*

With six feet left between them, Rafa and Marcus stopped. Rafa wondered, *What next?*

Darren spoke. "I'm so sorry." The appearance of his face and manner concurred with his words. He went on, "I hate this ugly war. I want it over. I wish I could turn back the clock. Rafa, you were my friend, and I let my childish attitude and ignorance lead to this. Your arm . . ." Darren's voice broke as he fought with his emotions. He hung his head, ashamed of his inability to control himself and more ashamed of the harm he had caused.

Rafa stood silent, his forehead tilted forward, while his eyes flashed below his dark lashes at the one who had sent that bullet flying into his elbow. His thoughts were racing. *I hate this man! How can I do this? But*

Marcus is right; I was doing the same thing he was doing. I was in the streets with my weapons and my hatred and my wrong motives.

A teaching from one of the Bible studies flickered in his mind: Jesus forgave His torturers. He thought, *I need to be more like Jesus, but I can't forgive him.* He looked at his sling and felt short of breath. He covered his face with his good hand. He prayed. "Lord, help me. You say, 'Forgive.' How?" The impossibility of forgiveness lingered in his mind as he stood beside Marcus with Darren barely more than arm's length away.

These three college friends became a silent, painful triangle, confused, not knowing what would come next. They could hear a couple dogs barking back and forth from the neighborhood next to campus. Three teenagers jogged by on the other side of the creek. The silence between them grew more than uncomfortable.

Marcus did not speak. He waited, and he prayed. His friends could not hear what he said, but he trusted his words reached the invisible realm of the Spirit. "Lord Jesus, send your power on us. Help us. In your name I ask for peace, your peace in all of us, right here, right now."

Then he spoke to his friends. "You two are world-changers. You are! You're doing it. You're fighting against these terrible forces that have brought us here. You're doing great things, and God is helping you. Some things we cannot do on our own. We can't forgive, not like Jesus did. But we can let Him help us do it. He's here. Life can change. Life can be better."

Fifty

Then, unbelievably, a miracle transpired right there on the trail next to the campus. The storm broke. The invisible violent winds quit. The unseen rough waves settled down. The broken, flesh and blood Rafa stepped forward through the inexplicable calm that settled over that spot on Putah Creek trail.

Rafa grew up hearing about his murdered uncle in Venezuela. He understood that he himself could have been cut down in the same manner here in California. Yet he reached out. He lifted his one good arm up from his right side and moved it forward with overwhelming grace and power toward a broken and repentant agitator. He wrapped that magnificent arm around the shoulders of the demon who destroyed his other arm.

He spoke quietly into the ear. "Darren . . ." He stopped; he searched for inner help. The spring breeze picked up. The birds chirped a little louder. The cheerful shouts of a few children playing downstream drifted through the air.

Darren waited, speechless, crushed into an undeniable humility by the current of spiritual power that flowed through the embrace of that good arm. He glanced at the awful black sling on Rafa's other incapacitated arm and quickly turned his eyes away.

Rafa started again. "Darren . . . I cannot tell you how horrible this has been. You can't imagine how hard it is to lose an arm. I hate it. I hate it! But I want you to know—you need to know this—I don't hate you. Not anymore. I did. I hated you from deep down in my gut, more than I've ever hated anyone or anything. But it's changing. I'm changing. I'm fighting with the sin of hatred. I'm getting better, but I could never have come this far on my own."

With his good arm still wrapped around Darren's shoulders, he continued, "I've turned my life over to Jesus Christ. He's real. He's powerful. He changes lives. He's changed mine. He changed Marcus and Hunter. Let Him change you. He can. He can give you a better life. Let Him into your heart."

Rafa let go, and Darren stood there and cried. The big, tough man who was going to fix the world with his arsenal of weapons wept brokenly. The only One capable of repairing the pervasive brokenness of the world was there, making His presence and power known.

"Okay." The word squeaked out of Darren's tearful face. "I want it."

Rafa said, "Then you have to do what Marcus made me do. Say this, 'Lord Jesus, come into my heart.'" Darren said it. It came out slowly. "Lord Jesus . . . ." Darren hardly understood what he was doing, but the power of the words and the arm that had embraced him were so completely convincing, he could not deny the reality. "Lord Jesus . . . come . . . come into my heart." "My heart"—as he said it, doubts filled his mind. He said, "Jesus would not want to come into this heart. It's not a clean heart."

Marcus spoke. "It's okay. None of us deserve His love. But He offers it. The debt we owe God for our sick decisions has already been paid.

Jesus did that on the cross. Now let Jesus do His thing. He wants you as His own, Darren."

Rafa took over. "Darren, say this. You need to say it. We all need to say it. 'Forgive me for all my sins.' And while you're asking God to forgive you, I want you to know this . . .." Rafa's next words got stuck in his throat, but he struggled and pushed them out.

"Darren, I . . . forgive . . . you."

Rafa had to stop. His emotions stirred, and he felt a heavy weight pressing on him, but it began to lift even as he spoke the words, "forgive you." He knew it would not be enough just to say the words. He had to follow through. It was right. It was from God.

As Rafa's gracious expression sunk in, Darren was again over-whelmed. It was hard to believe, but he knew Rafa well enough to know that he spoke from his heart. Darren knew he had to go forward with what Rafa and Marcus were telling him. So, with a voice slightly more solid than before, he said, "Forgive me . . . for all my sins."

Rafa spoke again. "One more thing. Say this: 'God, fill me with the Holy Spirit.'"

Darren balked. "How can I ask God to fill me with the Holy Spirit? Why would anything holy want to have anything to do with me? I'm about as unholy as you can get." A truthful but dejected look came over his face.

Rafa responded, "You're right. We're not holy, not at all, but the Lord chooses to give us the gift of the Spirit. It's not something we can earn."

Darren, still crestfallen stared at Rafa and then Marcus.

Marcus tried to encourage him. "Darren, listen, Jesus is called 'the Lamb who takes away the sin of the world.' When we believe in Him, we receive complete forgiveness. If God forgives you, you're forgiven, regardless of your opinion of yourself, regardless of what others think about you, and regardless of anything you've done."

Darren responded, "Really? That's . . . that's really amazing. I need to learn more about this." They knew he was feeling better when he added, "I'm a detail guy, you know." All three smiled, and Darren said, "Okay, what do I say?"

Rafa and Marcus answered simultaneously, "God, fill me with your Holy Spirit."

"Okay. Here goes." Marcus and Rafa listened as their old friend said, "I don't get this, but God . . . God, if You're actually listening to me, come on. Fill me with the Holy Spirit. I don't understand it, but I trust these two new friends of mine." He gazed from one to the other. Then with complete sincerity he said, "Thank you." He paused, looked directly into Rafa's face and said it again, "Thank you."

Fifty-One

During that summer Marcus spent as much time as he could with Darren, as much as Darren would allow. Darren was still Darren, but the Holy Spirit was obviously at work.

Fall came. The same conglomeration of churches planned another outdoor event. This time Habakkuk Band was not the back-up band, another group was. The organizers asked Elijah and Marcus to bring a great concert of praise and to sprinkle in a few inspiring, short talks between songs.

After dreaming, visioning and praying together, they agreed on a plan and called a huddle. Both Rafa and Darren agreed to meet Elijah and Marcus at the Black Bear Diner close to their alma mater. It was the restaurant where Hunter and Piper announced their engagement. The four arrived, sat down, ordered snacks and began to visit.

Soon Marcus announced, "We have an idea, a good one." Darren looked at Rafa and quipped, "This isn't the first time this guy's had a plan for us." Rafa smiled briefly, although he still found it difficult to smile around Darren. He also flashed back to the wilderness trips Marcus had conned them into.

Elijah nodded his agreement with Marcus, who went on. "Another unforgettable outdoor rally is coming up in October, early, like the sixth. Habakkuk gets to play. The organizers want our worship music, but they also want us to include a few short talks. We think the Lord wants you two"—both Darren and Rafa shot questioning, semi-defensive looks at Marcus, who said, "Just listen, think about it, and pray about it. You could come up together in between songs and share part of what happened between you. Not long, not all the details, just the basics. It's heartbreaking, but powerful. I'm sure you've both seen the incredible way people are affected when they hear it.

"We have a vision. We want people to worship Christ. We also want everybody to turn down the hate and learn to follow Jesus, who says, 'Love your enemies.'"

Darren breathed out, "Whoa, not sure about this." Rafa listened and tried to envision what it would be like to talk in front of that many people. They continued discussing the possibilities, and the Holy Spirit worked through Marcus and Elijah. Rafa came around first. Then Darren.

The band set up on the back of a flatbed truck that had a history of doubling as a stage. The platform faced the grandstand at Grant Union High. No Pacers game was planned for that Thursday night. The temperature was around 75 degrees, hardly any breeze, and the stars began showing up when the sun went down. A lovely night for a concert.

Apparently, Habakkuk Band was a good draw; 900 people filled the stands. Both Darren and Rafa were nervous. Marcus was excited. Elijah was prayerful.

The crowd connected with Habakkuk almost immediately. The band started with several well-known worship songs. They sang them wholeheartedly in a worshipful attitude. They shared a couple songs Marcus and Elijah had cowritten, which Habakkuk had recorded. These songs were quickly gaining listeners on social media and Spotify. Elijah and Marcus took moments in between songs to encourage the crowd to listen for God's voice.

During the last segment, Marcus started an introduction he had planned ahead of time. "We have a few more songs. It's been great to be out here tonight. We're blessed." He sensed and heard lots of affirmation. "Before we get to those last songs though, a couple of my best friends are here tonight, and I'd like to introduce them to you. Their story, their true story ought to be repeated over and over all across the country. So, if you want to record and share, go ahead. Here are my friends Rafa Milagro and Darren Hastings."

The two climbed up the metal steps and walked to the middle of the stage. Here and there throughout the crowd people began video recording with their phones. Rafa stepped up to the mic. "Hello. I have to admit I'm a little, no, a lot nervous. I've not done much of this, well, not at all." He looked out into the kind faces of strangers near the front and was reassured to a degree.

He gestured with his hand and said, "This is my friend Darren. We started backpacking together in college, over in Davis. We became good friends, even though he's very liberal in his politics." A few uneasy chuckles came up from the crowd. "I'm quite conservative. So, we didn't always get along.

"Then something terrible happened. The drummer in our band, The Yearning, was by the courthouse one morning observing a political rally. You might guess what happened in this crazed world we live in. A shot was fired. They hit Hunter. He was just standing there, not a political guy. He was just observing the crowd. He died from the wound a couple days later. I blamed the ultra-liberals for Hunter's death. So, I joined a militia to fight them. Darren, like I said, was a liberal." He looked at Darren and asked, "You ready to talk?"

Darren took Rafa's place at the mic. The crowd was quiet, attentive, captivated by what they heard from Rafa. "Well, like Rafa said, I lean left in my politics. So, I blamed the extreme right for killing Hunter, and I went to war. In my head I did. I joined a group that villainizes every conservative person on the planet. Our friend Hunter's death was a terrible, needless tragedy.

"Another senseless tragedy followed. I have to take responsibility for it. I was at a political rally one night at Howe Community Park. I was on one side of the street, the liberal side, and unknown to me, Rafa was with his people on the other side. I'm ashamed to say it, but I fired my pistol. I just shot into the crowd with no idea who was over there. It was absolutely wrong to shoot, I know, but here's what happened. My bullet hit Rafa."

Darren stopped. It was obviously difficult for him to voice the next sentence. "My bullet caused my friend to lose the use of his left arm. That's why he wears that sling." Darren hesitated again. A complete hush had fallen over the stadium. He started again. "You're probably wondering how the two of us could be standing up here together and talking about this. Can you take over here, Rafa?"

"Yeah." Darren stepped aside. Rafa took the mic, but he stood silent for a few moments before speaking. "I used to be a bass player. Marcus, the dude with the mint green guitar up here, he's been my friend since college, freshman year. I played bass in the band he started, The Yearning. I can't play anymore. There's so many things I can't do anymore. All this has been extremely hard to accept. Like Darren told you, he pulled the trigger, and he knows how horrible this has been for me. And yeah, you're wondering how we can stand up here together and share all this. It's not easy, believe me. It's a struggle, but there's one key that's made this miracle possible.

"Since the time he shot me in the arm, we've both accepted Jesus into our lives." The crowd reacted with gentle applause. "I hated him, and I could never have forgiven him for this." Rafa paused and prayed under his breath. Then he said, "I'm standing here, claiming Darren as my friend again because Jesus has taught me to do it and helped me follow through." He looked over and said, "Darren?"

As he walked to the mic, Darren hung his head and then stood silently before lifting his eyes to the crowd. "I asked Marcus to get Rafa and me together. We met on a trail beside the UC-Davis campus. We had only talked to each other for a short time before Rafa did an unbelievable thing. He came over close to me and put his one working arm around me." Darren had to stop. "He hugged me, like I was his friend again. At that point, about six months had passed since I shot him. But he forgave me, and he told me how to accept Jesus. He told me God forgave me and that Jesus was helping him forgive me. His actions and his words devastated me, but it was lifechanging. I will never go back to the hateful way I lived.

"I'm trying to learn to do what Jesus tells us to do. 'Love your enemies.' I thought Rafa was my enemy because of his politics. And really, our politics haven't changed. He's still conservative, and I'm still liberal." Darren lifted his voice slightly. "But we're not enemies."

Strong applause rose this time from the mesmerized listeners. Darren had to cry out loudly with his last words because of the clapping. "We will be friends and brothers in Christ for the rest of our lives." The people stood to their feet, still applauding.

Elijah approached the mic. Rafa stretched his good arm over toward Darren who reached back to him. They kept their arms around each other's shoulders as they walked off the platform. The people cheered. Some lifted their arms in praise to God. They continued to worship and cheer and clap their hands for several minutes after the two had disappeared from their sight.

Elijah spoke. "We don't need this civil war! We need to do what these two brave men have done. We can put this war behind us. We can learn to love again. We can forgive. We can work things out with one another.

"A movement is catching on from coast to coast and everywhere in between. I saw many of you recording Rafa and Darren with your phones. Forward it all over the country, all over the world! Let people hear. America is through with this hate.

"America has plenty of heroes, but today we desperately need men and women who will act like Rafa and Darren, peacemaking heroes. Why don't you choose tonight to be like them, to forgive, to reconcile? We can learn to be peacemakers. Jesus Christ will teach us how to do it." Confirming verbal affirmations and applause came from hundreds of people in the stands.

Marcus with his classic guitar and The Habakkuk Band returned to their places on the stage. They led the congregation in two more worshipful songs. Moved by the Spirit, those present throughout the stadium experienced an uncommon bonding with people they knew and with others they had never met. Many people kept envisioning Rafa reaching his good arm out to Darren. Following his powerful example, they reached out and embraced one another.

Marcus closed his eyes and flowed with the music and the moment. Caught up in the Spirit of the Lord, he saw the people as the calm surface of a peaceful blue sea. In that moment he heard a calling from God. "Go and speak to the storms and calm the turbulent waters. Wherever you go, be a peacemaker for Me."

Action Steps
To help Spread the Culture
of Christ-Centered Peacemaking

Pray.

Forgive someone who hurt you.

Love someone who seems like an enemy.

Post a review of this book on Amazon.

Encourage someone to read *Speak to the Storms*.

Invite the author to speak with a group at church or anywhere else about the culture of Christ-centered peacemaking.

Contact Ben at benwilliamsbooks.com, or brotherbenwilliams@gmail.com.

Other Books
By Ben Williams

Found at benwilliamsbooks.com

Forty Days in the Sierra Wilderness. Published 2017. Revised 2019.

This Moment with God. Published 2021.

Made in the USA
Columbia, SC
25 September 2024

42396334R00126